LAKSHMI and the RIVER OF TRUTH

A fairy tale for adults

Paul Chasman

Illustrations: Jerry Kruger

Paperback ISBN: 978-1-945587-73-3
Library of Congress Control Number: 2021919408

1. quests; 2. fairy tales; 3. philosophy; 4. hero's journey;
5. ocean voyages; 6. humor; 7. satire
Book design & production: Dancing Moon Press
Cover design & production: Dancing Moon Press
Illustrations: Jerry Kruger
Manufactured in the United States of America
Dancing Moon Press
dancingmoonpress.com

Bend, Oregon
Lincoln City, Oregon

DANCING
MOON
PRESS

CONTENTS

INTRODUCTION   5
1. WE SEE YOU   9
2. HEAD STANDS   15
3. LONG LEGS   25
4. IRONICALLY CHALLENGED   31
5. SPECIAL ED   41
6. A CONVERSATION   47
7. THE CLASSICAL ORATORS LEAGUE   55
8. LAKSHMI'S SPEECH   63
9. DOLDRUM BRIDGE   71
10. THE OTHERS   79
11. LOVE STORY   89
12. SPECIAL ED'S ADVENTURE   97
13. UNINTENDED CONSEQUENCES   109
14. METAPHOR HOTEL   119
15. MARK QUESTION AND THE QUESTION MARKS   131
16. TALK RADIO   141
17. SOPHIA ARRIVES   149
18. STORMING THE PALACE   155
19. MISTER BIGLY'S MANIFESTO   161
20. THE RIVER OF TRUTH   171
EPILOGUE   181

INTRODUCTION

FELLOW TRAVELERS, let us embark upon a journey into obscure caverns, steep ravines, unconscious mysteries, and cryptic conundrums that constitute the dream world of Lakshmi Jackson. Before we set sail into her deep domain, it will be useful to survey the seaworthiness of our vessel, plug the leaks, check the tarps, test for rope frays, and, as they say, batten down the hatches. If we are to achieve a thorough illumination of Ms. Jackson's inner landscape, we must take inventory of the various constructs we may encounter along the way.

For you 21st century pioneers who pursue the elusive vapor that is the human psyche, Sigmund Freud possessed the keys to the kingdom with which he opened the doors to understanding. In Freud's view, all human experience, including dreams, could be viewed through the lens of sexuality. If, for example, Lakshmi dreamed of eating a carrot, Freud would stroke his beard and explain that the carrot represented a penis. On the other hand, if Lakshmi were to report a dream about sniffing a rose, Freud would certainly interpret the rose as a symbol for…a penis. Even the above-mentioned boat, tarps, rope, hatches, as well as Freud's beard and the act of stroking it, are clearly metaphors representing the ubiquitous penis.

Freud's disciple and colleague, Carl Jung, broke with his mentor when he hypothesized that our dreams delve into the "collective unconscious." Jung posited that many icons we see and events we experience in dreams are universal symbols shared by all humanity. To illustrate the schism between Freud and Jung, if Lakshmi Jackson were to have a baby and the next night she dreamed about it, one might imagine the following dialogue between the two eminent psychologists:

Jung: My patient just gave birth to a baby.

Freud: *Mazel tov!* Please extend my warmest regards and give her this cigar as a token of my congratulations. Sometimes a cigar is just a cigar, although in this case, probably not.

Jung: She reports that last night she dreamed about her baby's birth. No doubt, she was tapping into the collective unconscious, summoning the universal metaphor of child birth to represent her personal metamorphosis from meek little clerk at the In 'n' Out Market to courageous national leader.

Freud: Nonsense! Dreams about childbirth clearly represent the penis!

Jung: I'll see you in the Court of Collective Unconscious!

(Author's note: The hypothetical example of Lakshmi bearing a child has no basis in reality. At this embryonic stage of our tale, Lakshmi Jackson has not given birth to a child, nor has she dreamed about it. These images are solely the author's musings employed as devices to illustrate the differences between Freud and Jung's thinking. However, they may lead the reader to speculate on this author's preoccupation with child birth, personal growth, and penises. To answer these complex questions would require years of analysis.)

Before Freud and Jung contributed scientific thought to Western dream doctrine, indigenous cultures around the world relied on shamans to guide them through a practice known as "vision quest." While it is impossible for us in the "civilized" world to wrap our rational minds around the concept of a vision quest, suffice to say it involves a spiritual guide who meditates, drums, chants, and personally enters the dreamer's nocturnal wanderings. We are left to speculate on how Freud and Jung would interpret a shaman in full spirit-warrior regalia, chanting and drumming as he makes his grand entrance into Lakshmi Jackson's aforementioned dream via her birth canal.

Freud's famous statement, "Sometimes a cigar is just a cigar," is only partially true. When we view a cigar under a microscope or under the influence of psychedelics, it is evident that a cigar is not a cigar at all. Rather, it is a living, breathing, floating universe of molecules; expanding, contracting, nudging one another, transforming, and creating the illusion of solidity. It is only a cigar because we have learned to identify it as such.

The point being, after 70 years of intense study which has included sleeping every night and dreaming during many of them, this author has determined that dreams are the figurative cigar under the microscope. Dreams are thought molecules that live, breathe, and float in the brain; expanding, contracting, and fluidly melding into one another to create new thought molecules.

How else to explain the conclusion of Lakshmi's aforementioned dream in which she was not visited by a shaman at all; rather, after giving birth to a baby girl, her thought molecules merged to transform her baby into an old man who, stroking his beard and lighting a cigar, declared, "Welcome to our collective unconscious."

With that, we are now sufficiently equipped to accompany Lakshmi Jackson on her epic quest to discover the River of Truth.

Let us begin.

"We See You"

1. WE SEE YOU

Wherein Lakshmi Jackson departs Red Rock seeking the River of Truth; sets sail in the Boat of Bob; falls asleep and is spirited away by ancient tribal guides.

WHEN LAST WE VISITED Lakshmi Jackson, she was extending a farewell hug to her dear tattooed friend, Sophia Wise, and setting forth on her Homeric odyssey to find a river in the Northwest Highlands. Having escaped with Sophia from the lethal clutches of tattoo artist-turned-megalomaniac, Roland Brand; having fled Capital City in "time" to elude Chosen Leader Delbert Thorne's misguided nuclear disaster; having escaped to the Southwest desert town of Red Rock which, due to nature's retribution, was now beachfront property; having, along with Sophia Wise, created a Red Rock sanctuary where fugitives from the Free Nation's coastal disasters could settle, heal, and begin new lives; and having celebrated her 20th birthday in fasting, silent meditation, and allowing Sophia to give her a fantastically kinky perm they spent half the night creating, Lakshmi began receiving nightly visitations from her dreamscape mentor, Virtuous Liar.

"Ask me a question; I'll tell you the truth and I'll tell you a lie," said he.

Virtuous Liar: endowed with the stature of a fire hydrant; shrubby gray beard reaching his waist on the left; right side of his face bare; skinny feet in long, brown, worn-out boots splayed at right angles.

"How will I know what you say is truth and what is a lie?" Lakshmi inquired, brushing her newly frizzy black hair from her curious chestnut eyes.

"You won't definitely not know!" he declared, laughing so hard he fell on his back, kicking his feet in the air, peddling an invisible bicycle.

"You ambiguously will!" He bounced to his feet. "It will become opaquely transparent. Maybe."

"I'm confused."

"*You're* confused," bellowed Virtuous Liar. "How do you think *I* feel? Can you imagine how discombobulating it is to say things like this all the 'time?' "

Their nightly conversations proceeded in this vein for a week. On the seventh night, Virtuous Liar climbed to the second rung of a ladder, and behind bushy brows, he stared Lakshmi meaningfully in the eye.

"Find the river, Lakshmi Jackson." He huffed and wheezed through flared nostrils. His nose hairs flapped like windblown leaves.

"Find the river and you will find the truth."

"That is not a lie?" she tested.

"The river tells no lies. Find it!"

And with that, Virtuous Liar evaporated into the fog of Lakshmi's sleep, leaving her in morning's first sunlight to ponder his parting words.

"Find the River of Truth," he had said. She knew not how, she knew not where, but find it she must, and find it she would.

"Somewhere in the Northwest Highlands," he had said.

She packed her knapsack with a cheese brick, a bread loaf, hat, gloves, and raincoat. She tossed the sack and a full canteen into the dinghy she'd borrowed from Bob, who once had been spiritual leader of the Free Nation and now was Red Rock's beloved maintenance man. She patched a leak directly beneath the vessel's name, *The Boat of Bob,* checked the oars for cracks, and unfurled the sail while her friend Ivan Bunt declared the boat to be in ship shop shape. Bidding tearful goodbyes to her loved ones, of whom there were many, she promised to see them again.

And with that, much like a more illustrious literary character in a more greatly acclaimed sequel, Lakshmi Jackson lit out.

*

It was a pleasant day. Mother sea gently rocked Lakshmi's cradle-of-a-boat, whispering her soothing oceanic song. The amiable morning sun warmed Lakshmi's bare brown shoulders and lifted her spirit as she peered into an azure sky adorned with cottony cumulus clouds. There was only this moment. No reflections on past disasters and loss; no fears of future perils; no needs, no chatter, no thoughts other than to be in this moment in "time," on this boat on this sea, hearing the vast ocean lapping, sails flapping, and the caw of a gull flying overhead beneath the sky and the clouds and the sun.

Lakshmi lay back and closed her eyes as her boat hypnotically swayed. Her thought molecules swirled and drowsily formed a musical ensemble: A bird soloing melodically over the harmonic changes laid down by an oceanic rhythm section; flapping sails and bouncing boat providing steady percussion in syncopated "time."

"Concerto in C Major for Bird, Ocean, and Boat" expanded and contracted in harmony with Lakshmi's new thought molecules that introduced a staccato wall of congas. From a small corner in distant "time" and space, a repetitive indigenous chant crept into the mix and joined the drums, first a distant whisper. Then, like an advancing army growing in strength and numbers, it marched to the forefront; a torrential crescendo building into a wall of pandemonium, drowning the oceanic orchestra and surrounding Lakshmi's consciousness with ancient heartbeat rhythms until the relentless primal mantra was all she heard.

Within the closed-eye darkness, faces materialized, disappeared, then re-emerged as near as lovers or kidnappers. Painted brown faces; archaeological ancestors adorned with elaborate jewelry, beads, and bones; taking turns speaking to Lakshmi with ebony eyes that bore into her, wordlessly saying: "We see you."

Out of the swirling fugue of tribal faces and "time"-less rhythms appeared long, rubberlike arms waving sinewy like seaweed on the ocean floor. They reached out to Lakshmi and laid on gentle but insistent hands.

"Come," the hands beckoned.

Lips did not move, hands did not drum, yet the cacophonous music continued. Only the prophetic eyes and rubber hands spoke in verbal chorus: "We see you."

Bodies took form: lithe bodies as dark as their eyes; dancing bodies; men and women with springy, elastic, boneless bodies clothed in animal hides.

Fluidly, Lakshmi's thought molecules morphed again, transforming her into a child—no, a baby—helplessly trusting the chanting elders who, like a stoic, pragmatic mother, collectively cradled her, caressed her, and carried her away:

Away across centuries of ocean.

Away across miles of "time."

Away beyond shape and form.

Away beyond design.

*

Lakshmi opened her eyes to find herself back in her young woman's body, sitting on the ground at the base of an enormous, old oak tree. The tribal chants pulsed in her ears like a distant, receding river. The faces were already a faded memory. Lakshmi's thought molecules had replaced them with a vast field of grass, split by two dirt trails forming a V, heading toward the horizon in two distinct directions. It was at the apex of the V that the solitary tree grew and where Lakshmi now sat at the crossroads.

She rose to her feet, looked around, and much to her surprise, her thought molecules brought before her a man. And he was standing on his head!

Hazel and Philbert Brain

2. ḢEAD STANDS

**Lakshmi meets the upside-down Brains;
has a first encounter with MISTER BIGLY;
is serenaded by a band of upside-down
bagpipers.**

WHEN LAKSHMI JACKSON rose to her feet, the upside-down man leapt backwards. The reader would be remiss if he, she, or however the reader identifies, were not to pose the question: "How does one, in fact, leap forward, backward, or any which way, while standing on one's head?"

The answer is, in this case: Quite well, all things considered. Accounting for the fact that the head contains no natural mechanisms such as toes, feet, ankles, legs, joints or muscles with which to propel the body in any direction, it must rely on an extremely flexible and durable neck to do the job. Lakshmi's thought molecules gave this man and his compatriots who would soon follow—long, strong, versatile necks.

The first of those compatriots was an upside-down woman who quietly materialized beside the retreating head-stander, utilizing the same mode of transportation as her companion. Tip-toeing would be a convenient if inaccurate depiction of her tentative entrance; it might be more aptly described as cranial-creep.

15

"Shh…" said the man, pressing his index finger to his lips. "This one stands on her feet," he whispered.

"Do you think she's an Other?" the woman asked.

"I don't know. Her complexion is quite brown. Maybe we should notify the authorities."

The man and woman circled Lakshmi wearily as one would surround an exotic animal, with curiosity and caution. Lakshmi noted nothing remarkable about the pair, other than the fact that they wore identical khaki shirts and pants, and they walked on their heads. She watched in wonder as they bounced around her front, sides, and back, becoming increasingly emboldened to examine her at close range. The woman was the first to reach out and test the fabric of Lakshmi's shorts. Upon doing so, she turned to her comrade and passed the following judgment:

"Feels real enough."

"Hmm," said he, while lightly nudging her leg as one would prod a baked potato to see if it was done. "Bend down, please," he requested of Lakshmi. "I can't reach your face."

Wishing to be polite, Lakshmi bent toward the man, but couldn't resist asking, "What on earth are you doing and why, by the way, are you upside-down?"

The two recoiled as if they had poked a rattlesnake. "The question is," said the woman, attempting to regain her composure, "why are you standing with your feet on the ground while your head is on top? And while we're at it, why are you wearing pants?"

"But you're wearing pants too," Lakshmi replied.

The couple exchanged perplexed glances.

"But isn't it obvious?" said the man. "Oh dear, I really think she doesn't know. Hazel," he said, turning to his partner, "we'd better explain quickly to this poor girl before the authorities come."

"Authorities?" questioned Lakshmi.

"Listen, my girl," the man said furtively. "It is quite evident that it would be impractical for my wife to wear a dress. If she were to do so, it would fall over her face.

"Conversely," he continued, "before MISTER BIGLY decreed that we be turned upside-down, he required that dresses be mandatory for foot walking women."

"MISTER BIGLY?"

"You don't know MISTER BIGLY?! My stars, this is worse than I thought. But first, please excuse me for being so rude. I haven't even introduced myself. My name is Brain. Philbert Brain. This is my wife, Hazel."

"Nice to meet you, Mr. and Mrs. Brain. I'm Lakshmi Jackson. But…"

"No 'time' for buts, Lakshmi Jackson," interrupted Brain. "You'd better stand on your head before MISTER BIGLY finds out."

"But who is…"

"Let me explain," said Brain. "We don't have much 'time' before the pipers arrive."

"The pipers?"

"Long ago," Philbert Brain continued, "when we were still foot walkers, we were allowed to make our own decisions."

"There was a 'time' when we women foot walkers didn't even have to wear dresses. Until we did," added Hazel Brain.

"The thing we love about MISTER BIGLY is, he's so honest," said Philbert. "Most people lie, but pretend they're telling the truth. MISTER BIGLY tells you he's lying."

Lakshmi's thought molecules conjured up an image of Virtuous Liar. "Always remember, Lakshmi Jackson," he admonished, "there is a big difference between being open and being honest." Then he vanished.

Philbert: "MISTER BIGLY's motto is, 'There's a sucker born every minute.' "

Hazel: "He claims he made that one up himself."

Philbert: "Which proves he's right because we believe him."

Lakshmi interjected. "Do you believe he made it up, or do you believe there's a sucker born every minute?"

"Exactly!" Philbert exclaimed. "Now do you see how MISTER BIGLY turned us upside down?"

"Well…"

"MISTER BIGLY made his fortune when he founded MISTER BIGLY's Institute of Higher Greed where, for an astronomical fee, students were taught the secret to becoming obscenely rich. The answer being, of course, to open an Institute of Higher Greed and charge astronomical fees."

"Don't forget the golden thrones," reminded Hazel.

Lakshmi's thought molecules that made Hazel mention golden thrones blended with new thought molecules that brought MISTER BIGLY to the forefront, speaking to an unseen audience from a television screen. He was sitting on a sparkling gold toilet.

The Elvis hair was coal black, as if it had been painted with shoe polish, (which as the reader shall soon learn, was exactly the case). The pompadour stood a good six inches straight up, then abruptly jetted out at a gravity-defying 90-degree angle for another six inches, providing umbrella-like shade over his shifty eyes. The sideburns were long, wide, and flared like bell-bottom pants, nearly reaching his downturned lips.

(If MISTER BIGLY were to smile, the sideburns might have touched the top corners of his lips, but there was as much chance of him smiling as of him getting a joke.)

The suit jacket was powder blue and adorned with glittery gold patterns. The long tie continued this motif with a golden MISTER BIGLY inscription running vertically from his chest all the way to his otherwise exposed nether parts which did not require much area of the tie to cover.

At first, Lakshmi thought MISTER BIGLY's thin mustache looked like a caterpillar, until upon closer reflection, she realized it was a caterpillar! It stretched and contracted like an accordion as he spoke directly into the TV camera:

"Today, I'm announcing my terrific new line of MISTER BIGLY'S Tremendous Golden Thrones. Lots of people say they're tremendous! Believe me! By the way, how tremendous are they? Look at this."

He lifted his tremendous 400 pounds up from his golden toilet, and Lakshmi's thought molecules revealed that he wore no pants at all. Was this an oversight on MISTER BIGLY's part, or a deliberate distraction from the flimsiness of his message? Hard to discern, but Freud, no doubt, would have had the predictable interpretation.

MISTER BIGLY went on. "My tremendous toilets … err … thrones… are solid gold! Now you can look as rich as me! Hell, you can be as rich as me! Buy ten of them and sell them to your friends! I'm giving 'em away at a bargain basement price of $500,000 each. Turn around and sell 'em for a million bucks a piece and do the math! You'll be tremendously rich! Believe me!"

But MISTER BIGLY wasn't done. "And if your MISTER BIGLY Tremendous Golden Throne gets worn out, I've got just the thing for you."

He held up a can of yellow paint.

"This is my tremendous line of MISTER BIGLY's Tremendous Golden Gloss. Just slap a coat of this stuff on your throne and tell your sucker friends it's solid gold! You can con them just like I'm conning you now!

"But wait! There's more," he continued. "For an extra thousand bucks, I'll throw in a bottle of MISTER BIGLY's Tremendous Shoe Polish and Hair Dye! Everybody knows you can't pull off a scam without matching hair and shoes! Many people say that! Believe me!

"Just remember my motto: Buy MISTER BIGLY's Tremendous Products! They Are What They Are!"

And with that, the thought molecules that had washed MISTER BIGLY in swept him away, and in washed Hazel and Philbert Brain to pick up precisely where they had left off. Hazel again:

"And then he told us about the Others."

Philbert: "Yes, the Others. MISTER BIGLY explained that the Others are not like us, and we must be very scared. The Others come in a variety of colors. They're dirty and dangerous. They have no morals and they want to destroy our way of life."

Hazel: "Not only that, they're poor!"

Philbert: "MISTER BIGLY explained that if your skin isn't a natural Free Nation flesh tone, you're poor. If you're poor, you're a loser. He said if we love humanity, we must exterminate the Others. They're losers."

Hazel: "So he turned us upside down."

Lakshmi thought: "I'm brown. Check. I'm poor. Check. My feet are firmly planted on the ground. Check. I must be..."

Philbert: "You're getting ahead, Hazel. First, he made us take this pledge (Philbert and Hazel recited together):

Black is white,

Night is day,

There are no doubts

Or shades of gray.

Blood is green,

Grass is red,

Truth makes sense

When stood on its head.

"And that's when he made us stand on our heads."

"And told us we could identify the Others because they were the ones who were standing on their own two feet," explained Hazel.

"Which is why," Philbert concluded, "you'd better stand on your head right away, Lakshmi Jackson, or risk being exterminated."

*

As Lakshmi pondered the Brains' dire warning, a bizarre sound emerged from some distant corner of the horizon. A high-pitched drone that, as it approached, revealed itself to be quite annoying.

"The pipers!" Philbert and Hazel Brain exclaimed in unison.

Lakshmi peered toward the source of what might be loosely described as music and viewed on the two trails that converged in a "V," two approaching lines of bagpipers bouncing on their heads.

The mechanical execution of bagpipe performance (or "pipes") requires an extraordinary amount of effort resulting in minimal reward. The piper (sometimes generously referred to as a "musician") blows a vast amount of air into a bag and regulates the flow by employing arm pressure, all the while somehow manipulating the melody pipe, or "chanter" with both hands. The fruit of the piper's labor is a sound not unlike a swarm of wasps after one has thrown a baseball into their hive. Scholars have noted that one can distinguish one bagpipe song from another by the name.

As the aforementioned pipers descended the converging trails, Lakshmi was able to identify the song they played as *Danny Boy*. The fact that they were marching on their heads compounded the degree of difficulty, with each head bounce causing a hiccup in the melody, contributing to the overall irritating effect of the rendition. If lyrics had been added to the whining melody accompanied by the incessant tonic drone, it might have sounded like this:

Oh, *Danny Boy* (hic)

The pipes, the (hic) pipes are call-(hic)-ing

From glen to (hic) glen (hic)

And down the (hic) mountain (hic) side (hic)

Etc... (hic)

"The pipers are here! The pipers are here!" cried the exuberant Brains, holding hands as they danced on their heads around Lakshmi as if she were a May pole.

"Come with us and join the pipers!" they called and disappeared into the rapidly approaching, deafening bagpipe parade.

As the pipers emerged into stark relief, it became clear that they had not eschewed their traditional garb, a staple being the plaid skirt-like cloth known as a kilt. Given that the pipers were upside-down and as convention would have it, no undergarments were included in their attire, the kilts fell over their chests, rendering their nethers exposed, once again leaving Lakshmi's thought molecules ripe for Freudian interpretation.

Lakshmi stood by the base of the old oak tree at the apex of the diverging trail, now surrounded by bouncing, head-standing pipers who made such a hiccupping racket, she could barely hear herself think. But her thought molecules did manage to tamp down the noise long enough to allow Virtuous Liar's admonishment to seep anew into her consciousness:

"There's a big difference between being open and being honest."

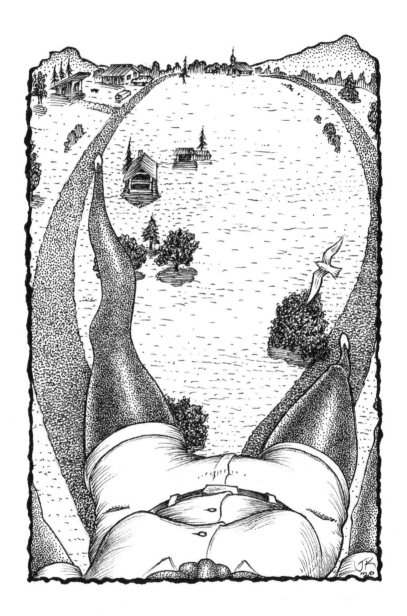

"Lakshmi found herself, quite literally, with her head in the clouds."

3. LONG LEGS

A brief discussion of history's most profound song; a rumination on the relative reality of life and dreams; Lakshmi follows the pipers and beyond on impossibly long legs; finds herself at the doorstep of a most unusual hospital.

OPEN YOUR BOOK OF BOB to Chapter VIII, page 119, and read from Dad's Book of Children's Verses 1:1, the lyric to the most profound and prophetic song in the history of Western Civilization:

Row, row,

Row your boat,

Gently down the stream,

Merrily, merrily,

Merrily, merrily,

Life is but a dream.

Granted, the author's judgment may appear subjective. The reader may argue that "Heartbreak Hotel" rivals *Row Row Row Your Boat* for its depth and erudition. A powerful case can also be made for *Please Please Me*, *Only the Lonely*, and *Walk Like a Man*. *La Bamba* is in the running. However, after careful scientific study, the conclusive evidence proves beyond a shadow of a doubt that *Row Row Row Your Boat* is hands-down the most sublime and Zen-like statement ever set to lyrics and music.

(Note: This study does not account for cowboy songs, which must be considered in a separate category. In this genre, the indisputable evidence points to *El Paso* being the greatest cowboy song ever written, while *Ghost Riders in the Sky* remains a respectable if distant second.)

But, for Lakshmi Jackson, the unresolved existential question posed by *Row Row Row Your Boat* remains: Is life but a dream? And conversely, is this dream in which she is immersed, but a life? Or, are life and dreams fluid with one another, co-existing simultaneously, like parallel yet overlapping galaxies? Or, to put it another way, how do life and dreams identify: "He/him"; "she/her"; "they/them"; "it/id"?

To address these weighty questions, we cannot ignore the conspicuous truth that Lakshmi's life as well as her dreams are the product of some random thought molecules floating in the brain of an old fart sitting at his laptop, racing to stay one step ahead of depression.

But dear reader, please don't minimize those floating thought molecules. If you do, you might as well minimize your own life. For what *is* your life but your own perception of it? And what are your perceptions but a bunch of thought molecules shifting and changing and rolling around like a kaleidoscope in the chemical soup you call your brain?

Be that as it may, when the band of pipers led Lakshmi through the meadow on the "V"-shaped trail, that moment was more true for her than the "reality" that she was sleeping on a boat. And how, you might ask, did she manage to traverse a trail that veered so sharply in two distinct directions? Quite effortlessly, it turns out. For, you see, in this moment her thought molecules gave her inconceivably long legs!

Lakshmi found herself, quite literally, with her head in the clouds, revealing a splendid aerial view of her feet straddling the two trails a quarter mile below. Although her body remained its familiar size, her elastic legs wobbled and stretched like two spectacular tentacles. While the rival bands of pipers competed to lead Lakshmi on their chosen trails, they quickly became required to address a more urgent concern, which was to avoid getting squashed like ants.

Not that Lakshmi wished them harm. Especially now that their piping was little more than a distant whisper, she no longer felt a temptation to grind them violently into the ground. No, she walked oh-so gingerly to avoid smashing the scrambling pipers underfoot. Fortunately, this tenuous circumstance was short-lived, as, after a few giant strides, she had outdistanced the pipers and left them to their own devices, to their own thought molecules, if you will, far behind.

So much for the road less traveled. Most often in this dream we define as "life," we are forced to choose our metaphoric path, only to wonder what we missed in the road not taken. But Lakshmi's long legs spared her the agony of such decisions. Her thought molecules afforded her the luxury of having it all.

*

It was a sunny yet cool day, and Lakshmi took great joy in her journey along the two trails. Her heightened vantage point enabled her to view the world from a fresh perspective. The trail leading east passed through thick green woods alive with birds, deer, and wild flowers. The western trail led down a steep ravine where, at the bottom, lay heaps of oil cans, plastic bottles, and rusted car carcasses. Lakshmi's eagle eyes surveyed every detail below: To the east, the leaf turning gold, the insect burrowing in the ground. To the west, she read the label on a discarded bottle: "MISTER BIGLY'S *Tremendous Shoe Polish and Hair Dye.*"

The trails continued to diverge, requiring Lakshmi's legs to stretch some more. She grew so tall that her head peeked into the blue sky above the clouds. She ducked as a jet flew overhead.

Reveling in her newfound height, Lakshmi leapt forward, first with her left leg, then with her right. Upon her first jump, she secretly smiled. Then she grinned. Then she laughed out loud as she sprang as if on pogo stick legs, ecstatically covering huge swaths with every bound.

"Time" and space are difficult concepts to define in our waking thoughts. They are even more elusive in dream world. Therefore, we will not attempt to measure the distance Lakshmi traveled in her long-legged mode, nor will we mark the "time" she spent in frolic. Suffice to say, she traveled great distances and it took a while.

Gradually, the trails began to merge, and correspondingly, Lakshmi's legs began to shrink. Once again, she found her head below the clouds and her body gently descending toward earth. By the "time" her legs returned to their accustomed size, she paused at the confluence of the converging trails. And there before her stood a sprawling, crumbling, antediluvian building, appearing like a 19th century insane asylum. Over the giant wooden double front doors hung a sign that proclaimed the following:

HOSPITAL FOR THE IRONICALLY CHALLENGED

"Good day, Lakshmi. So ironic that you're here."

4. IRONICALLY CHALLENGED

Lakshmi meets two doctors at the Hospital for the Ironically Challenged; attends a support group for white-haired white men; has a close call from which she is rescued by an unexpected visitor.

DOORS ARE MADE to be opened, especially in dreams. So, it should come as no surprise to the reader that the heavy wooden doors to the Hospital for the Ironically Challenged swung open, and Lakshmi floated in.

Inside the stone-cold foyer, Lakshmi looked straight ahead, then to her right, then to her left, and saw long halls stretching in all three directions. The dingy corridors were lined with door after metal door, each monocled with a barred window at head level. Every door stood closed and silent.

"Good day, Lakshmi Jackson. So ironic that you're here."

Two doctors, a stout woman and a short, balding man, each wearing a white smock and headband mirror, greeted her with open left hands extended. The somewhat overbearing woman appeared to have large pillows stuffed in every region of her garb. She spoke:

"I am Dr. Drole. This is my colleague, Dr. Farse. Welcome to the Hospital for the Ironically Challenged."

"Nice to meet you, Dr. Drole, Dr. Farse. I just…"

"We've been waiting for you. You're late." She glanced at her watch.

"No matter. Now that you've *finally* arrived, it's high 'time' we take you on a tour of our facilities. But before we introduce you to our patients, we must orient you with our practice in order that you grasp the gravity of our purpose. A good place to begin is with our mission statement."

Dr. Drole pointed to a plaque, prominently exhibited in a glass display case on the foyer wall. It read:

"We, at the Hospital for the Ironically Challenged, are committed to healing the afflicted who, whether due to congenital condition or willfully closed eyes, are blind to irony, satire, and absurdity. A debilitating side effect of this tragic disease is a confounding inability to recognize metaphor, allegory, simile, parody, or humor. These deficiencies manifest themselves in a myriad of symptoms, but one common trait shared by every wretched soul who is diagnosed with Ironically Challenged Disorder (ICD) is an inability to recognize irony within his or her own self. Our mission is to heal our brethren through education and sensitivity training when possible, and to protect the public from these individuals when their pathology is beyond redemption."

"We find it ironic…" Dr. Farse began.

Dr. Drole finished his sentence. "…that you would be visiting our hospital. As I recall, your best friend, Sophia Wise, constantly interrupted you and would never let you finish a sentence."

"Well, yes, that's true, but…"

"And now you come here and find yourself confronted with the same dilemma. Isn't that ironic?"

"I suppose that…"

"Don't disrupt my train of thought, Lakshmi Jackson! There's nothing so ill-mannered as someone who tries to get in a word edgewise while I'm speaking. As I was saying to Dr. Farse yesterday, 'There are too many speakers in this world and not enough listeners.' And he was like, 'That's a valid point.' And I was like, 'And they totally go on and on with a whole lot of blah blah blah without saying anything at all.' And Dr. Farse was like, 'Well said.' And I was like, 'Shut up, Dr. Farse! I'm talking! As I was say-ying, brevity, Dr. Farse! I'm all about brevity! The world would totally be a better place if people would learn the art of brevity!' "

"So true," volunteered Dr. Farse.

Lakshmi: "It does seem ironic that…"

Dr. Drole: "Ironic? You want to see ironic? I'll show you ironic! Our ICD support group is beginning its session. Come with me."

Lakshmi's thought molecules wafted her with the doctors into a large windowless room with a chalkboard in front, cluttered bulletin board in back, and pictures of MISTER BIGLY on the walls. A dozen or so white-haired white men dressed in identical suits and ties sat in a semi-circle behind first-grade classroom desks. One of them was speaking:

"…and furthermore, my organization, the Anti-Science Society (ASS) has determined through rigorous scientific study, that science is a hoax. I just think…"

"Mr. Dunst," this was Dr. Drole speaking, "has it occurred to you that what you are saying is pathologically ironic?"

"Dunst has a point," said a white-haired white man by the name of Jolly. "My company, Men Of Reason Or Not (MORON), was on the verge of proving climate change doesn't exist. Then a hurricane blew our office down."

"Tell us more, Mr. Jolly," replied Dr. Drole.

Mr. Jolly continued. "I ran out of the way of the collapsing building and got hit by an ambulance."

"Go on..."

"My wife and I went for marriage counseling, but we had to stop. Our counselor was getting a divorce."

Dr. Drole turned to Lakshmi. "You see what we're up against."

Dr. Farce suggested, "Mr. Parr, we haven't heard from you yet. Would you like to tell the group what's on your mind today?"

Mr. Parr was a white-haired white man. "I am a man of faith. I believe in a just and merciful God. Human life is sacred. That's why anyone who takes a human life should be put to death."

"Mr. Parr," said Dr. Drole, "do you recognize the irony in what you are saying?"

Mr. Parr: "Irony? Never heard of such a thing."

Dr. Drole: "Mr. Blunt, would you like to explain the meaning of irony to Mr. Parr?"

Mr. Blunt, a white-haired white man, said this: "I'll take a stab at it. I believe in family values. Marriage is a sacred institution between a man and a woman. Sodomy and adultery are abominations."

Dr. Drole: "Mr. Blunt, I will remind you, you were caught in a rest room stall with a young boy. What does that make you?"

Mr. Blunt: "A fiscal conservative."

Another white-haired white man, Mr. Glum, spoke up: "Fiscal conservative, my keister! Everybody knows you sold your MISTER BIGLY *Tremendous Toilet Paper* stocks on a tip the day before they went belly up!"

"I'll have you know that MISTER BIGLY's *Tremendous Toilet Paper* is considered to be the highest quality sandpaper by carpenters throughout the land! And another thing..." began Mr. Blunt, but Dr. Drole cut him off.

"Would someone like to comment on the irony of this conversation?" she asked.

"I would." This was Mr. Balance, a white-haired white man. "But we're ignoring the elephant in the room," he continued. "We're discussing trivial matters in the midst of a crisis! Police are murdering unarmed black men at an epidemic rate. They've been strangling them with choke holds, suffocating them with hoods, and shooting them in the back. Murder is wrong! Why don't they simply maim them?"

"Exactly right!" exclaimed Mr. Grumble, a white-haired white man. "Our police are the innocent victims of brown people who prey on them with their cell phone cameras!"

Dr. Farse: "All right, gentlemen. We've had our therapeutic conversation. It's 'time' for the lightning round. Dr. Drole will make a brief statement and you will say the first word that comes to your mind. Are you ready?"

"Ready."

Dr. Drole: "Okay. Here we go. The citizens are in a rage. They've taken to the streets to peacefully protest the cruelty and inequities of their government. They're shouting, carrying signs, making speeches, and demanding justice. What do we call them?"

"Socialists!"

"Anarchists!"

"Traitors!"

"Okay. Next question. In response, busloads of counter-protestors armed with guns, machetes, and assault rifles scream racial slurs, attack the demonstrators, and provoke a riot. What do we call them?"

"Freedom fighters!"

"Patriots!"

"Good people!"

"Let's try another one. A terrible disease infects and kills millions around the world. MISTER BIGLY sells his line of *Tremendous Peroxide* which he claims, when injected with his line of MISTER BIGLY's *Tremendous Syringe and Needle Kit*, will not only cure the disease but will turn the skin a 'tremendous shade of white' from the inside out. What do we call this?

"Free market capitalism!"

"Unorthodox leadership style!"

"$24.99 for a 12-ounce bottle!"

"One more. MISTER BIGLY keeps a harem of two dozen women. He bulldozes historic churches and replaces them with a chain of box stores called MISTER BIGLY's *Tremendous Drive-Thru House of Worship*, which look like a cross between the Taj Mahal and a fast-food burger joint. His friends are dictators and gangsters; his enemies are the poor, the afflicted, and the Others. He claims superiority of the white race, although his skin is clearly orange. He earns a dollar for every lie he tells, which makes him a billionaire many 'times' over. What do we call MISTER BIGLY?

"An imperfect messenger!"

"Guardian of religious freedom!"

"Protector of Democracy!"

"There you have it, Lakshmi Jackson. You can see for yourself how tragically handicapped these people are. And what about you? Are you able to recognize irony when it hits you over the head?"

"Well," she began, "I guess I do find it a bit ironic that while I'm searching for the River of Truth, I instead find myself wandering through a dream in which people are turned upside-down, my feet stretch to impossible lengths enabling me to walk down two paths simultaneously, and now I'm visiting an institution ironically named the Hospital for the Ironically Challenged."

"Ironically named?!" cried Dr. Drole. "I'll have you know there is nothing ironic about this hospital! We take our work very seriously! I take my *self* very seriously! This is solemn business, Lakshmi Jackson, and I assure you there is nothing ironic about my mission to cure my tormented patients of their irony deficit! I have dedicated years of study to this illness and I guarantee you, I am the world's leading authority on irony. Ask me any question on the topic and I will give you the definitive answer."

"Is there such thing as a definitive answer?" Lakshmi asked.

"Of course there is!" bellowed Dr. Drole. "And the definitive answer is no."

"Excuse me, but isn't that ironic?"

"Are you questioning me, young lady? I'm beginning to think that you might be ironically challenged yourself." Dr. Drole's voice took a menacing turn. "Let's see if a few years in our hospital won't cure your deficiency."

And with that, Lakshmi found herself surrounded by a swarm of white-haired white men who descended upon her, singing loudly, out of rhythm and out of tune like a tone-deaf family at a birthday party:

"THIS LAND WAS YOUR LAND,

BUT NOW IT'S MY LAND!

I TOOK IT FROM YOU,

AND NOW IT'S MY LAND!

THIS SONG DOESN'T RHYME,

AND I DON'T HAVE TO!

THIS LAND'S FOR THOSE WHO LOOK LIKE ME!"

They grabbed her and pawed her and pinned her to the ground. One white-haired white man seized her arm while another white-haired white man brandished a bottle of MISTER BIGLY's *Tremendous Peroxide* in one hand and MISTER BIGLY's *Tremendous Syringe and Needle Kit* in the other. He was preparing to inject it into her vein, when suddenly there commenced a wild chaos of shouting, snarling, growling, barking, and biting. The white-haired white men parted like the Red Sea in another fairy tale from long ago.

The white-haired white men were gone. Dr. Drole and Dr. Farse were gone. And taking their place before Lakshmi stood a handsome black lab, smiling, wiggle-waggling, and very happy to see her.

"Bud!" she cried. "I thought I'd never see you again!"

"Bud?" exclaimed the dog. "You know Bud died in the last book. My name is Special Ed."

"Special Ed's job is to take care of his humans."

5. SPECIAL ED

Lakshmi meets a talking dog; he offers his specialized assistance on her quest; they experience a merging of thought molecules; she discovers the perfect skipping rock.

SPECIAL ED SIDLED UP to Lakshmi in the vacated Hospital for the Ironically Challenged and bonked his head affectionately on her leg. "Oh please please pat the head!" he declared.

Lakshmi patted his head.

"Oh please please scratch the back!" he said. His dripping tongue dangled out of his smiling mouth. How could she resist?

"Oh oh now the chin! Oh yes the chin! I do so very much enjoy the chin!"

He wiggle-waggled enthusiastically as Lakshmi rubbed and patted and scratched. Special Ed was so very happy to receive all this loving attention, but he might have been even happier if he had gotten just a little bit more.

"You missed a patch by my ear," he said.

(Author's note: Whenever "he said" is written in reference to Special Ed, the reader may infer that it could have been written as: "he said enthusiastically." In order to avoid redundancy and to save paper, the author invites the reader to fill in the blanks.)

"Thank you for protecting me, Special Ed," Lakshmi said.

"Most assuredly! That's Special Ed's job." He rolled on his back and curled his front paws. "The tummy, please. Please scratch the tummy."

Lakshmi obliged. "Your job?"

"You're my human," he replied. "Special Ed's job is to take care of his humans."

Lest the reader think Lakshmi was surprised to encounter a talking dog, kindly be reminded that she had borne witness to Bob who regularly conversed with his dog, Bud. While she never actually heard Bud speak herself, it was evident that Bob did. Further, as Lakshmi swam in her thought molecule soup, such a trifle as Special Ed having command of the English language posed no obstacles to his credibility.

He prodded her out of the meeting room and into the hospital lobby.

"Make a hurry, Lakshmi! We haven't a momentum to lose!"

"Hurry? For what? To where?

"Why, the River of Truth, most assuredly! Isn't that what we're seeking for?"

"Well, yes," Lakshmi said. "Do you know where it is?"

"Most assuredly I do not. But Special Ed will help you find it."

Lakshmi silently mused. "This dog is lovable enough, but I can't imagine how he can be of any help."

"That's easy!" said Special Ed. "It's the smeller."

"Your smeller? Wait a minute! I didn't say anything, but you answered my thoughts."

Special Ed smiled and leaned all his weight into Lakshmi's legs. "The neck, please. Kindly scratch the neck."

He continued: "Most assuredly, the smeller! It's much smarter than yours. Special Ed can smell things you never imagined. If your smeller were a penny, mine'd be a hundred bucks."

"And so..." Lakshmi began.

"And so, I will find the River of Truth with the smeller. Most assuredly! C'mon! Let's make an excaddadle!"

"Wait a minute," Lakshmi balked. "How did you read my mind a minute ago?"

"I didn't read your mind," said Special Ed. "What makes you think a dog can read?"

"But..."

"I just listened to your brain. Our thought molecules must have gotten mixed up together. That usually happens sometimes."

Lakshmi was intrigued. "Let's try again. I'll think a thought and you tell me what it was."

"Okay. On your mark, get set...think!"

Lakshmi closed her eyes and visualized a waterfall: a clean cascade of melting snow from the highlands, tumbling and splashing white into a sparkling green-blue lagoon below. She imagined picking up a rock along the bank and skipping it. The rock flitted along the surface like a firefly, too fast to count the skips, then dived to the bottom and disappeared.

"Oh boy oh boy!" cried Special Ed. "You're going to throw me a ball!"

Lakshmi opened her eyes. "Hmm," she said. "That was close, but..."

"Try again," said Special Ed.

43

This "time" when Lakshmi shut her eyes, she imagined looking down by her feet, and there she spied the most flawless skipping rock in existence: round as a globe, flat as a frisbee. She picked it up—the perfect weight. She rubbed her fingers over the smooth, skin-like surface.

"Throw me the ball! Throw me the ball!" yelled Special Ed.

When Lakshmi opened her eyes, she held the skipping rock in her hand.

"Throw me the ball!" he yelled again.

He crouched in front of Lakshmi with his backside pointing straight up. He nudged her ankle and pointed down with his nose. Lakshmi glanced to where Special Ed's snout was aiming, and there by her feet on the hospital floor, much to her astonishment, lay an orange tennis ball!

Only one thing to do. She threw the ball.

It flew through the open doors and far outside the Hospital for the Ironically Challenged. Special Ed sprinted after the ball and passed it as it rolled. He doubled back, and in one commotion, he corralled it and skidded along the path as he swooped it up in his mouth. Then he dropped it where he had found it, albeit covered with slobber, and bounded back to Lakshmi.

"Throw it again, Lakshmi! Throw it again!" He bounced and panted and grinned.

But Lakshmi had other things on her mind as she exited the hospital. For, she slipped her hand into her right pants pocket, and there she fingered the world's most flawless skipping rock.

"I mustn't waste this perfect rock on a casual skip," she thought. "I will save it, and one day I'll find the perfect 'time' and place, and I will skip it perfectly."

"I know she's going to throw Special Ed the ball," he thought. "Most assuredly!"

So, with their thought molecules intertwined, Lakshmi and Special Ed ventured forth, new partners in their quest for The River of Truth.

"Throw me the ball!"

6. A CONVERSATION

Lakshmi and Special Ed proceed on their journey; a discussion ensues regarding goals, Special Ed's job description, and the Others; Special Ed elucidates some definitions; they make a pact.

ℌAVING DEPARTED the Hospital for the Ironically Challenged, Lakshmi and Special Ed headed north by northwest, with Special Ed leading the way. The terrain they traversed was a continuation of the grassy meadow that had led Lakshmi to the hospital, sans the trail. Special Ed would lope alongside her, nosily sniffling the ground, trotting ahead to scout out the next uncharted territory, then returning to Lakshmi to report his findings. Occasionally, he sprinted out of sight to chase a squirrel or a rabbit, but Lakshmi quickly learned that he would inevitably circle back, happily wiggle-waggling, empty-handed so to speak, happy to have participated in a sport while unattached to the outcome—which became a point of inquiry for Lakshmi.

"Special Ed," she asked, "have you ever actually *caught* a squirrel?"

"Nope," was his reply.

"Do you expect you ever will?"

"Nope."

"Then why, pray tell, do you chase them?"

"You see, Lakshmi," he explained, "we dogs are most assuredly different from you in that way. When I first began to learn your language, there was one word that stumped me. It's a word that still has me fuddled, but I think Special Ed is getting close. That word is: 'goal.' "

He continued. "If people had a dollar for every goal they aimed for, you'd all be millionaires. Me? When there's food in front of me, I guess you could say my goal is to gobble it up as fast as I can before somebody else gobbles it up. But once I start in, I'm too busy gobbling to think much about it.

"When I'm tired, my goal might be to have a nice snore. Maybe I have a goal to find a soft bed, but usually I can find a place that's soft enough. Or not."

"What about when you're chasing a squirrel? Isn't it your goal to catch it?" Lakshmi asked.

"Hmm…" Special Ed considered the concept. "Never thought of it that way. That's a curious way to look at it. Not sure what I'd do if I caught him. I just like to run real fast and follow his zigs and zags, and when he runs up a tree, I like to jump on the trunk and yell, "Come on down here and let me chase you some more!'

"I guess you could say my 'goal' is to have fun. Most assuredly."

He turned the thought over on its side and upside down. Then he added, "I don't know if that's an actual *goal*, actually. Special Ed just sort of has fun because it's fun to have fun."

As if to prove his point, a squirrel scurried before them, and Special Ed sprinted away to give chase.

When he loped back, smiling and wiggle-waggling, Lakshmi continued the conversation.

"But isn't it your goal to help me find the River of Truth?"

"I wouldn't say it's my exact *goal*, exactly," he explained. "It's my job."

"You said it was your job to take care of me. What did you mean?"

"Don't you know?" he asked. "It's because Special Ed feels so sorry for you."

"Sorry for me?" She was quizzical. "Why on earth do *you* feel sorry for *me*?"

"Cause of what we were just talking about, silly Lakshmi! You're loaded down with so many goals! Your poor brain is stuffed full of bothers! *What's right? What's wrong? What should I do with my life? What am I here for? What is the meaning of life? Should I have cereal or pancakes for breakfast?*"

"And you don't think about those things?"

"Not muchuva lot. Ask me what I'm thinking right now."

"Okay, Special Ed. What are you thinking right now?"

"I'm thinking pancakes. Yup. Most assuredly pancakes for breakfast."

"Is that *all* you're thinking?"

"Thinking? Umm...I dunno. Let me think about it. Umm...let's see...I'm walking with you...we're having a nice chatter...I sniffle grass and earth and worms and... somebody peed here yesterday..." Special Ed lifted his leg, peed on the spot, and sniffled some more.

"I think it was a rabbit...maybe a pregnant mother...Yes! Most assuredly a pregnant mother! I forget—what was the question?"

"What are you thinking about?"

"Right. Now I'm thinking about the upside-down people you met. They thought you were an Other."

"That's right! How did you…"

"That was when I *knew* I had to take care of you. You *are* an Other, and I'm an Other too."

Lakshmi sensed the truth of what he said, but she didn't quite understand. "Tell me more."

"You, Lakshmi, are an Other because you're a brown-skinned woman in a white man's world. You love birds and trees and flowers in a world full of cars and trucks and things that go."

Lakshmi was reminded of her father who read her a book by that name. She felt a pang of sadness as she recalled Ben Jackson and his ignominious demise.

(A refresher course on The Book of Bob will remind the reader that Ben Jackson was a loving and devoted father until he was driven mad when Roland Brand drove Lakshmi's mother Aruna mad with his brainwashing. Ben became The Roadside Slaughterer who ruthlessly murdered many innocent people in his ill-fated attempt to impose revenge on Roland Brand. The story did not end well for Ben Jackson, aka: The Roadside Slaughterer.)

"I'm so sorry about your father," said Special Ed. "But, as I was saying, you never cared much about cars and trucks and things that go. You're more curious about hearts and minds and things that feel. You aim for the truth, Lakshmi. In a land where people stand on their heads, you stand on your feet. That makes you an Other."

"And why are *you* an Other?" she asked.

"Me? Is your smeller *that* bad? I'm a dog!"

"And…?"

"Do you know what 'experts' call it when I cry because my people are packing their suitcases?"

"I give up."

" 'Conditioned response.' "

Special Ed continued. "It took them years of doing scientific research on us to figure that one out. Which reminds me, do you know what they call it when humans are especially mean to each other?"

"Tell me, please."

" 'Inhuman.' Do you know what they call it when people are inhuman to animals?"

"What?"

" 'Scientific research.'

"Lakshmi, do you remember when you faked throwing me the ball and I chased after it, and you laughed and laughed?"

"I'm sorry, Special Ed," She giggled. "But you have to admit you were pretty funny."

"I guess I was. But do you know why, no matter how many 'times' you faked a throw, I chased it again?"

"Because people are so much smarter than dogs?"

"There are lots of kinds of smarts, Lakshmi. I just happen to be really smart at being honest. How could anybody be so stupid as to lie? That's another word I don't quite understand: 'lie.' No matter how many 'times' you fake me out, I trust you because I believe you're wonderful. Isn't Special Ed smart?"

"I suppose when you look at it that way..."

"Do you know what humans call a dog who acts like a human?"

"No...?"

"You call him a 'good dog.' Do you know what you call a dog who acts like a dog?"

"A bad dog?"

Special Ed leapt on his hind legs, leaned his front paws into Lakshmi, and bowled her over as he slurped her a kiss on the face. "You get it! Most assuredly you get it!" he cried. "Special Ed knew you would!"

Then he ran three very wide circles around Lakshmi and plopped himself in front of her, belly flat to the ground, tongue hanging out of his smiling, panting mouth.

And with that, Lakshmi and Special Ed agreed to make a sacred pact to which they would both swear. Lakshmi's thought molecules produced a rolled-up scroll of the finest quality paper. When she opened it, there displayed before her in exquisite calligraphy was the oath they both recited:

"I (Lakshmi Jackson/Special Ed), vow to be your teacher, student, protector, and friend. I will always speak the truth to you, and I will never treat you like an 'Other.' I will never follow orders from you nor will I require you to obey."

"And I will never call you a 'good dog' or a 'bad dog,' " Lakshmi improvised.

"And I promise to never call *you* a 'good dog' or 'bad dog,' either," promised Special Ed.

The pact was immediately put to the test when Lakshmi said, "Okay, let's shake on it."

Special Ed balked at the suggestion. He pointed out that after centuries of dogs being ordered to "shake" like some cheap carnival trick, it hit a sore spot to be told by his human to "shake." The entire agreement appeared in jeopardy until Lakshmi proposed the following:

"Why don't you tell *me* to shake?"

Special Ed thought for a moment and said, "According to the new rules, I'm not allowed to *order* you to do anything. But I suppose if I ask nicely…. Okay, here goes: Lakshmi, shake!"

"I guess that was nice enough," she said. She held out her hand and he shook it.

Then Special Ed dropped a ball at her feet and said, "Throw me the ball! Throw me the ball!"

Lakshmi picked up the ball and threw it as far as she could. And this "time," she didn't fake a throw.

"Get on this ladder and climb down to earth!" the man
demanded.

7. THE CLASSICAL ORATORS LEAGUE

Lakshmi and Special Ed fly; encounter Wendell Smarm; attend a curious meeting.

LAKSHMI FOUND IT quite wonderful, though not unusual, to be flying. Special Ed too, reveled in his role as a flying dog. However, at this moment, he chose to be a passenger, sitting attentively on Lakshmi's back and allowing her to take the proverbial driver's seat. With his hair and ears pinned by the wind, he judged the experience to be every bit as rewarding as a car ride with his head out the window.

Swooping over fields and valleys afforded them a bird's eye view of humanity's legacy below.

"Look!" exclaimed Lakshmi. "There's a housing development!"

Sure enough, as they cast their eyes downward, they gazed upon a man-made monoculture: a perfectly organized aggregation of rooftops, row after row after row, each row collected in squares, each square a symmetrical Leggo village divided by bustling gray rivers of motorized ants, rushing every which way to god-knows-where.

Lakshmi's thought molecules gave her telescopic eyes which enabled her to read the street signs below. Streets with names like:

"Polar Bear Lane"

And:

"Spotted Owl Drive"

And:

"Grey Wolf Avenue"

"It appears the inmates have escaped from the Hospital for the Ironically Challenged," declared Lakshmi.

"Look!" said Special Ed. "There's another housing development!"

"How do you know it's not the same one?" Lakshmi inquired.

This was a legitimate question, for as far as Lakshmi and Special Ed could see, and for as long as they flew, there appeared to be nothing below them but one vast burb.

"I dunno," was Special Ed's answer. "But that remembers me a Zen question: If a tree falls in the forest but there's no more trees to hear it, does it become another housing development?"

"Good question, Special Ed. But there's only one housing development. It just never stops."

"Ya can't stop progress," said Special Ed.

But then again, maybe you can. Or so they would learn when they encountered an organization that was determined to try.

*

Gliding among the birds, Lakshmi and Special Ed reveled in their ethereal voyage. They swooped and soared, executing figure eights, backflips, and any manner of aeronautic maneuvers. While in the midst of performing a tandem Yurchenko double pike, they heard a rather urgent voice, calling from the clouds.

"Come down from there! Come down immediately! What in heaven's name do you think you're doing?"

Looking in the direction of the voice, they viewed a man merely a few feet in front of them, perched atop an improbably tall ladder. The top hat was black, as were the 19th century suit and shoes. The rosy bow tie provided a stark contrast to his pasty complexion. Lakshmi noted that his hands gripping the ladder were soft and pallid. They appeared to have never responded to demands greater than lifting a quill pen, which she would soon ascertain to be a credible observation.

"Get on this ladder and climb down to earth!" the man demanded. "You have no business flying up here!"

"But flying is such a joy, sir. When my body flies, my soul flies with it."

"Who said that? Was it Yeats? Whitman? Possibly Blake? I can't seem to place it. It's not familiar to me."

"I suppose it's quite possible that someone else may have said it first. But if so, I'm unaware. I just said it."

"*You* said it?!" exploded the man. "What business do *you* have saying something that hasn't been said before?"

"I don't know," said Lakshmi. "I just…"

"It's not even written down," grumbled the man under his breath.

"My friend Lakshmi can speak whatever she pleases," Special Ed chimed in.

"Oh," scoffed the man. "And I surmise you just made that up too?"

"Most assuredly," said Special Ed.

"I suggest you two climb down this ladder and come with me. We're going to be late for the meeting."

"Meeting?" said Lakshmi. "What meeting?"

"Why, the Classical Orators meeting, of course. Come! Hurry!"

Lakshmi and Special Ed obeyed their instructions and began a lengthy descent with their new acquaintance in the lead, several steps below them.

"Given your ignorance of my identity and stature, I suppose it would only be polite for me to introduce myself," huffed the man as he stepped gingerly from rung to rung. "My name is Wendell Smarm and, of course, I am President of the Classical Orators League."

*

Smarm led our duo down the ladder which, upon arriving at a rooftop, appeared to protrude unobstructed through the surface. Smarm did not hesitate. No, he continued to descend as if sinking in quicksand until he disappeared beneath the ceiling. Lakshmi and Special Ed locked eyes. She shrugged, he smiled and wagged his tail, and the two followed suit.

Upon sliding seamlessly through the roof, their eyes were greeted by an auditorium packed with people seated in folding chairs. The object of their attention was a singular man standing on a wooden podium perched on a stage. Rather short, balding, and sporting post-Civil War formal attire similar to that of Wendell Smarm, this man known as Archibald Snark addressed his audience in a most solemn and earnest manner.

"Tonight, I will read Patrick Henry's *Parson's Cause Speech* of 1771. I'd had thoughts of reading his 1775 *Virginia Convention*

Speech in which he famously said, 'I know not what course others may take, but as for me, give me liberty or give me death.' But I presume we all agree, that is such a tedious cliche! In the spirit of originality, I will opt for the more obscure but far more substantial *Parson's Cause*."

Mr. Snark gathered himself with a deep inhale, held it for three seconds, slowly exhaled through his lips, cleared his throat, and began.

"Mr. President. No man thinks more highly than I do of the patriotism, as well as abilities, of the very worthy gentlemen who have just addressed the House."

Snark plodded along in this vein until Lakshmi's thought molecules fast-forwarded to Patrick Henry's climactic finale:

"Do they feed the hungry and clothe the naked? Oh, no, gentlemen! These rapacious harpies would, were their power equal to their will, snatch from the hearth of their honest parishioner his last hoe-cake from the widow and her orphan children her last mich cow! The last bed—nay, the last blanket—from the lying-in woman!"

Archibald Snark stepped off the stage to a sprinkle of polite applause. Lakshmi and Special Ed watched from the back of the room as Wendell Smarm made his way to the podium.

"Thank you, Mr. Snark," he said into the squeaking microphone. "I commend your flawless technique, your sensitive phrasing, your impeccable attention to detail. You have accurately interpreted the author's intention.

"Next up, we have Priscilla Primbottom who will read Ralph Waldo Emerson's 1838 *Divinity School Address*. Ms. Primbottom will demonstrate that, yes, many women are capable of reading speeches too. Ms. Primbottom?"

Following Priscilla Primbottom was Matthew Cubbins' stirring rendition of Martin Luther King's *I Have a Dream* speech. Although a bit too contemporary and emotionally charged for the League's sensibilities, they received it courteously and with open minds.

Next up was Theobold Herrington advocating for a William Jennings Bryan Tribute night. The issue was hotly debated and voices were raised. Herrington's proposal revealed a deep split among the League pitting William Jennings Bryan's enthusiastic boosters versus the smaller faction that objected to Bryan's dispute of Darwin's evolution theory.

The League threatened to devolve into controversy when Wendell Smarm took to the stage and interrupted the proceedings with the ping of a small hand bell.

"We will revisit this debate at our next meeting," declared Smarm. "I will now call upon Lakshmi Jackson to read for us. Which famous speech have you prepared for us, Ms. Jackson?"

Lest the reader surmise that Lakshmi was taken aback by Smarm's surprising summons, we must remember that in her dream state, the extraordinary could be rendered unremarkable; the outlandish made mundane. Inhabiting a landscape in which she could fly with her talking dog, descend from the heavens on a ladder with a strange little man, slide seamlessly through the roof where she encountered a preposterous gathering called the Classical Orators League—is it any wonder that Lakshmi found herself on stage delivering a speech as matter-of-factly as if she were spreading peanut butter on toast?

"Ladies and gentlemen: Hear my plea!"

8. LAKSHMI'S SPEECH

Lakshmi addresses the Classical Orators
League; receives decidedly mixed reviews.

STANDING at the podium, Lakshmi surveyed the League
and began:

"Ladies and gentlemen: Hear my plea!

"Since 'time' immemorial, human beings have been stumped
by one puzzle they've found impossible to solve; one
overriding question that has gone unanswered. It is the
enigma that should haunt each of us, and the conundrum
that troubles me tonight. To state it plainly:

"How, in God's name, did it happen that, while the
human race is capable of so much love, kindness, and
creative beauty, we are so disposed to blind hatred, horrific
destruction, and unspeakable cruelty?

"How can it be that the same species that gave us
Michelangelo, Mozart, Lincoln, and Harriet Tubman, has
also produced Timothy McVeigh, Jeffrey Dahmer, Hitler,
and Atilla the Hun?

"How is it that we, who create stunning works of art, invent
cures for diseases, commit selfless acts of sacrifice in the
service of kindness, morality, and higher purpose, also cause
monstrous suffering at the hands of our insatiable addiction
to war, power, and greed?

"How can this dichotomy be? To paraphrase an old song: 'When will we ever learn?'

"Could it be that the contradiction between our animal and analytical selves is too great to reconcile? Are our conscious and unconscious minds, in the end, incompatible? Dare we imagine that we are simply a worthy experiment gone tragically wrong?

"Our ape ancestors are known to be warlike, to form tribes that commit atrocities and murder upon their brethren. What if *they* had the means to build sky scrapers and cities and empires? What if *they* had the intelligence to invent nuclear weapons and the means to implement them? Well, here we are.

"I will concede that we handle our responsibilities better than many species would. Can you imagine if *cats* had nukes? No doubt, the world would be a wasteland. For that matter, can we think of any being on this planet who should be entrusted with such an awful power? Well…maybe Special Ed, but I can't think of anybody else."

Lakshmi studied the room, allowing space for amusement toward her attempt at levity, however, aside from Special Ed smiling and wagging his tail at the mention of his name, there was not so much as a titter. Her audience studied her scrupulously. She continued.

"We've been given the ability to procreate prolifically and keep ourselves unnaturally alive until we're crowding every other species out and our planet is bursting at the seams.

"We've replaced nature with an artificial world of machines and concrete and steel. We've extracted the oil, clear-cut the forests, polluted the air, and depleted the ocean, all to perpetuate the illusion that we're making the world a safer, more comfortable home for ourselves.

"How can we, who are so smart, be so stupid? How can we, who extend so many extraordinary acts of kindness, be so selfish? Maybe the great Kurt Vonnegut had it right when he declared our age to be: 'The Era of the Great Big Brain.' He posited that humans were too clever for their own good, and he foresaw a 'time' when, as a survival mechanism, we would evolve into less intelligent beings, thus more viable.

"However, while there are unintended consequences to our sophistication, I cannot reconcile myself to humans' *intentional* cruelty. We all are taught: 'Do unto others…' We all subscribe to: 'Thou shall not kill.' We all have a conscience and we all have a soul. Yet we actively engage in or tacitly support actions that vandalize and destroy. Over and over and over again.

"We're smart enough to devise elaborate rationalizations for our actions. We divide up into teams and blame the other side. We imagine ourselves to be victims who must be vindicated. Or we simply give way to anger, fear, and revenge.

"Or we go to sleep. We swim in the shallow end of the pool where gratification equals fast food, new toys, and 'likes' on social media.

"I reject the notion that we are all prone to cruelty and violence; that we all are composed of equal amounts of brutality and kindness; that under the right circumstances, any one of us would inflict the electric shock if ordered to.

"As we know, it takes much 'time' and labor to build a house; it takes but one match to burn it down. Let us commit tonight to the hard work of building our house and renouncing the shortcut of destruction. Let us pledge that we will use our heads and hearts in tandem; that we will employ our intelligence to *serve* our better nature rather than to rule it; that, with every decision we make, we shall consider not only what is best for ourselves but what is best for every living being with whom we share this beautiful planet."

Then Lakshmi's demeanor shifted and she appeared to enter a trance. Her eyes gently closed; her head and body swayed; her arms floated in descriptive rhythm to her sing-song chant:

"I dream a world where wisdom reigns
and rains upon us
washing us clean:
clean of cruelty,
clean of hate,
clean of fear;
where wisdom's rain instructs us
to live our better nature,
to live in balance
with the earth,
with each other,
with ourselves;
instructs that we are primitive animals
with complicated minds—
instructs that in order to become
our elusive promise
we must use our genius
to heed our mammal wisdom,
guiding—not taming—the beast;
instructs that heart and mind must reconcile,
must integrate,
must live in concert
if we are to actualize our potential
and survive.
I dream a world where wisdom reigns.
I hear it raining grace;
I hear it raining harmony;
I hear it raining love.
Listen."

*

Lakshmi's speech was greeted with stunned silence. And not for the reasons the reader might surmise. The audience was not rendered mute by the dramatic impact of her message. The members were not awestruck by her emotional oratorical power. Rather, they were shocked to hear a speech they'd never heard before. It was left to Wendell Smarm to break the spell.

"That speech is foreign to me. Whose was it?" he asked.

"Why, it was mine," said Lakshmi.

"*Yours*? I don't understand. Let me ask another way: Who wrote it?"

"Nobody really. I mean, I never wrote anything down. You asked me to speak, so I spoke."

"Wait a minute!" The concept of a contemporary woman speaking her original thoughts extemporaneously caused Smarm's brain to convulse with cognitive dissonance. "But, are you saying you just made it up?"

"Yes," was Lakshmi's honest answer.

"Where's the transcript?" queried Archibald Snark.

"There is none, sir," she replied. "I just said what I thought to say."

"And what business have you, young lady," asked Priscilla Primbottom, "to make up your own speech? Don't you find it a bit presumptuous to put yourself in the same category as Plato, Disraeli, Cromwell, or King?"

"I don't put myself in any category, ma'am. I simply spoke my truth."

The League buzzed with agitation.

"If this young lady can make up her own speeches, what's to stop others from doing the same?"

"People could go around saying any old thing."

"Where is the respect for the classics?"

"Why, she didn't even employ formal diction!"

This last critique sparked a whole new round of controversies: Did she practice proper vocal warm-ups prior to delivery? Did she make appropriate use of the microphone? Were her timber variations in keeping with classical principles?

In sum, the League unanimously concluded that Lakshmi had disregarded tradition, flaunted her originality, relied excessively on emotion, and that she had fatal flaws in her technique.

So distressed were the League's members by Lakshmi's affront to their "time"-honored practices that they were at a loss as to how to proceed. It was left to Wendell Smarm to lead them out of the wilderness.

"Very well," he cleared his throat. "Speaking next, we have Baron Bland. What will you be reading for us tonight, Mr. Bland?"

"I will read from Socrates' *On His Condemnation of Death* speech, circa 399 BC."

A murmur of approval spread through the ranks, as well as a palpable sense of relief that the League was back on familiar ground. Baron Bland took his place at the podium, straightened his bow tie, performed a few neck stretches, closed his eyes for a meditative moment, took a deep breath, exhaled, and began.

*

At this point, the author is tempted to remark, "As the Bland played on…" However, this would be a cheap little joke that would contradict the seriousness with which the League members took themselves. So, we will resist that temptation and merely state the following:

As Bland droned on, Lakshmi and Special Ed stood in the back of the auditorium, becoming quite drowsy from the stuffiness in the air. They scanned the room, and ascertaining that the audience was fully engrossed in the immortal Socratic lyrics, they glanced at each other, nodded heads in agreement, and silently slipped out the ceiling from which they came, leaving the Classical Orators League to fulfill its sober mission.

Doldrum Bridge

9. DOLDRUM BRIDGE

The author opines on the concept of "time"; Lakshmi and Special Ed find themselves on a most unusual bridge; Lakshmi's disposition descends into what might be colloquially described as an "existential bummer"; a conversation ensues involving "time" and the purpose of life.

*

Author's note: It likely has not escaped the discerning reader's attention that, in this text, whenever the word "time" is written, it is surrounded by quotation marks. This practice pays tribute to the fact that "time" is a human-created construct which is, in reality, an illusion. This premise is magnified by our dream states, during which the custom of marking "time" by standard measurements such as seconds, minutes, hours, and years becomes rather superfluous. Further, one might posit that, in recognizing the ambiguous nature of "time," dreams offer a more accurate depiction of reality than the linear fantasies with which we deceive ourselves in wakeful consciousness. Because our story takes place within a dream, the author has opted to remain consistent with that modality by surrounding the word "time" with quotation marks. Without further explication, it is "time" to continue our tale.

*

UPON MAKING a furtive exit from their encounter with the would-be statesmen, Lakshmi and Special Ed slinked out through the auditorium ceiling. No sooner had they stepped into the open air than they found themselves standing on a seemingly endless footbridge extending far beyond their vision. The bridge appeared to be suspended by cables bolted to a billowy caravan of dark and heavy cumulonimbus clouds floating in the charcoal sky. As the clouds drifted, the bridge traveled with them, slowly meandering in tandem with the canopy.

Our protagonists were well-advised to walk gingerly on the weathered wooden planks in order to avoid stepping through the crumbling surface. The degree of difficulty was compounded by the absence of guardrails, leaving Lakshmi and Special Ed to monitor their every step like a pair of tightrope walkers lest they plunge off the edge into a dense sea of fog.

And if they were to fall, there was no indication of how far they would descend, for glancing below, they saw nothing but a swirling grey abyss. Forward, back, and down, the bridge disappeared into the same murky shroud. Only the overhead storm clouds and the bridge that danced like a puppet on wires revealed anything resembling shape or form.

So they walked. And walked. Scenery and circumstances remained unchanged. So they walked. Wondering if they had advanced anywhere at all. They walked. Trapped on rickety Doldrum Bridge, prisoners of empty "time," adrift in hollow space.

As they walked, Lakshmi's mood darkened. The colorless domain drained her of passion; bled her of hope; deposited a dull, leaden boulder of grief upon her chest. The answer to the existential question, "What is the meaning of life?" came down to this:

A doldrum bridge

in a doldrum fog

permeating Lakshmi's doldrum soul

which embodied doldrum grey

on a bridge that led to

DOLDRUM

She could not taste, smell, or feel; could not speak; could not cry; could not penetrate the void. She might have been a surgery patient, dull with anesthesia; or a sleepwalker dreaming within a dream. Somewhere within her, the boulder weighed oppressive with profound sorrow. It was too heavy to lift.

The task of translating Lakshmi's elusive turmoil was left to Special Ed who, upon absorbing her melancholy, was overcome with sadness. He whimpered, then cried, then howled for every pain his beloved human had ever endured. He sang her song of mourning over fate and loss and death. As dogs will do, he mirrored every nuance of cloaked emotion that her two-legged companion was unable to express.

Special Ed could not comprehend the source of Lakshmi's anguish. He couldn't understand Lakshmi's growing recognition of her fleeting existence and her woeful insignificance; couldn't fathom her witness to the world's suffering and her despair at her inability to change it; knew nothing of the hopes she'd had for her fellow humans which now lay buried in a graveyard under a rubble of arrogance, stupidity, and greed.

No, Special Ed knew none of these things, nor did he need to. He understood on the most elemental level, the depth and breadth of Lakshmi's vaulted grief. So, he cried.

*

They walked. And walked. As mentioned in this chapter's preface, the concept of "time" is problematic even in the most concrete of circumstances. It becomes exponentially more elusive when drifting in a dream. Having established this premise, it is impossible to calculate how long Lakshmi and Special Ed walked futilely on Doldrum Bridge. It is adequate to surmise that by their measure it took a long "time."

At some point in "time," Lakshmi came to this realization: The bridge they found themselves on was a conveyor belt that traveled in the opposite direction from which they walked—at precisely the same speed. As she and Special Ed attempted to proceed forward, the bridge revolved backward, rendering them frozen in place. She tried to run, but the bridge sped up in the opposite direction. She stopped, and the bridge stopped. She took a step backward and the bridge rolled forward.

Attempting a new tactic, Lakshmi pulled a ball from her pocket and threw it as far as she could. Special Ed leapt ahead as if to chase it, but the bridge matched his pace and he ran in place. Meanwhile, the portion of the bridge Lakshmi stood on remained stagnant. The ball rolled back to Special Ed and he snatched it up.

They were stuck. Paralyzed and depressed, Lakshmi did the one thing of which she was capable: She lay down on her back and blankly stared at the colorless sky. Special Ed wagged his tail and licked her face.

"Get up, Lakshmi!" he cried. "We have to make a go!"

"Nowhere to go, Special Ed. Nothing to say. Nothing to do. We're stranded forever on Doldrum Bridge."

Special Ed pondered that thought for a moment. Then he wagged his tail, licked her face, and said, "Get up, Lakshmi! We have to make a go!"

Lakshmi was rather annoyed by Special Ed's wet tongue. Wiping the slobber from her cheek, she rolled over on her side and exclaimed, "Don't you get it? We're stuck. We can't go forward. We can't go back. We're sentenced to a lifetime of prison on this godforsaken bridge, in this godforsaken gloom, in this godforsaken world!"

For the first "time" on Doldrum Bridge, Lakshmi's anguish spilled to the surface and she began to cry. "We're doomed, Special Ed! We'll be marooned on this bridge for eternity!"

"Get up! Get up!" cried Special Ed, clambering all over her and licking her face some more. "We have to make a go!"

She sat up and crossed her legs. "Where do you think we're going to make a go to, Special Ed? There's no way forward, no way back."

"There's more than one way to spin a cat, is what I always say. You just have to think outside the clocks."

"Don't you mean *skin* a cat? Isn't it think outside the *box*?"

"No no no," replied Special Ed. "If you say, 'think outside the box,' you're not thinking outside the box at all. If you say, 'think outside the *clocks*,' *now* you're thinking outside the box! Plus—you're not getting fooled by the trick of 'time,' which might maybe get you somewhere. Some 'time.' "

Special Ed's novel theory got Lakshmi to wondering what "time" it actually was, so she stood up, reached in her pants pocket, and pulled out a watch. Much to her surprise, there were no numbers on the face, and the hands stuck out, pointing directly at her.

"You see, Lakshmi," said Special Ed. "Now you're thinking outside the clocks."

When Lakshmi pulled the "time"-less watch from her pocket, she also discovered the flawless skipping rock she'd found on the day she met Special Ed and was saving for the perfect occasion. But in her current state of hopelessness, it was just a dumb rock cluttering up her pocket. She contemplated throwing it away.

"Don't do it!" implored Special Ed.

She stood up, fingering the rock. "What's the point?" she asked.

"The point?" Special Ed laughed. "The point? Don't you know, Lakshmi? There *is* no point! Do you think when I chase the ball you throw, there's a *point*?"

"I had such high hopes," sobbed Lakshmi, "that one day I would find the perfect place at the perfect 'time' to toss my perfect skipping rock and watch it skip perfectly across the perfect surface. I would make a perfect wish before my perfect throw, and the rock would skip a thousand skips and my wish would come true. But now…"

"Now…" Special Ed finished her thought, "you put that rock back in your pocket and save it for that perfect day. Then you throw me the ball."

"But all is lost. *We're* lost."

"Well, you know what they say: 'All who wander are not lost,' " Special Ed replied.

"Yes, but some who wander *are* lost. You said it yourself: There *is* no point."

"Lakshmi, if there *is* no point, then there is no point in throwing away your magic skipping rock. Put it back in your pocket and throw me the ball. PLE-E-EASE?"

Surrendering to self-pity, Lakshmi carried on the following conversation with herself:

"So, what did you do with your life, Lakshmi Jackson?"

"Why, I led a very productive life—I threw a ball for Special Ed."

"My, what an interesting life you've led! What other contributions have you made to humankind?"

"Why, I threw sticks for Special Ed too."

"What a wonderful human being you must be, Lakshmi Jackson!

"Oh yes, I have fully actualized my potential and am now the ball and stick thrower which I have always aspired to become."

"PLE-E-EASE throw me the ball?" Special Ed pleaded.

"This is pointless," said Lakshmi.

"You have a point. Throw me the ball!"

Still holding the "time"-less clock, Lakshmi rubbed her perfect skipping rock between thumb and forefinger and slipped it back in her pocket. Then she absentmindedly tossed the clock over the side of the bridge. But to her dismay, Special Ed jumped off after it.

"Oh no!" cried Lakshmi. "Special Ed!" And with that, she hurtled off the side of Doldrum Bridge in pursuit of her friend.

As luck would have it, Lakshmi's thought molecules gave her and Special Ed umbrellas which when opened, sufficed quite nicely as parachutes. Our two heroes came in for a soft landing out of the fog and were immediately greeted by a warped wooden sign nailed to a post planted firmly in the ground. The sign read:

BEWARE! YOU ARE ENTERING THE LAND OF THE OTHERS

10. THE OTHERS

Lakshmi and Special Ed enter the Others'
"re-education center"; they are treated to a
welcoming ceremony; Una tells Lakshmi the
history of the Others and warns her about
MISTER BIGLY; Lakshmi meets a handsome
prince.

FIRST, THEY SAW the cobblestone street littered with
tarps and tents; sleeping bags worn, torn, and soaked
with rain; rusty pots on open fires; kindling shards pulled
from wooden tables and fence planks; piles of muddy rags
that had once been clothes; shredded lawn chairs, rickety
and collapsed; tattered rainbow flag, once proudly flown,
now laying trampled in the dirt; bicycle carcass, belly-up,
tires flat, going nowhere; cracked and silent radio, electric
cord curling loose and plugged into air; plastic ukulele, its
busted strings popping every which way; plastic bottles,
plastic tags, plastic straws, plastic bags; whiskey and wine
bottles, empty and broken; a worn-out shoe; an unused
bus token; injection needle, drained and abandoned like a
praying mantis who, having mated once, got his head bitten
off for his troubles and now lay dead in the dirt. Broken
monuments to broken lives.

Next, they saw the children. Ragged and dirty, they
swarmed Lakshmi and Special Ed, barefoot and begging,

some hoping to sell pencils or trinkets, some simply holding out empty hands. With assorted skin shades of brown, blue, red, and green, their hungry, haunted eyes asked a silent question. Each with an "O" burned into his or her forehead.

An animal parade straggled forward: Grunting hog sloshed through the mud, eyeing them with mild interest; bedraggled horse nuzzled up to Lakshmi, hungrier for food than affection. A wary pack of wolves inspected Special Ed with bristled backs, but sensing no threat they moved on. Lions and tigers, eagles and sparrows, sheep and bears. Lakshmi would have thought she was visiting Noah's ark, but for the emaciated condition of every beast and the selfsame "O" displayed on every brow.

The adults finally emerged, tentatively at first; then the entire village filed out of their shelters. They surrounded Lakshmi and Special Ed, inspecting them with heedful curiosity. When Lakshmi reached out her open hand, they leapt back as one, then cautiously moved forward again. Like the children, their clothes were rags and their complexions revealed every color in the rainbow.

"Surely," thought Lakshmi, "these people would be quite beautiful if they weren't so starving and bedraggled."

Also like their children and the animals that preceded them, every citizen exhibited an "O" on his or her forehead. These were the Others.

*

"Come," said the ancient toothless woman, a murmur of a smile illuminating her otherwise stoic countenance. Lakshmi beheld the matriarch in wonder as her wrinkled blue skin melded into green, then to red, then to gold. Taking Lakshmi's hand, the woman led her toward the center of town. The villagers followed, then formed a semi-circle around Lakshmi and Special Ed.

"We are the Others. You and the dog are Others too," said the woman. "We embrace you."

The welcoming ceremony began with percussion. Congas, tablas, tambourines, tom toms, bongos, and snares sprung into the villagers' spirited hands which shook the ground with a persistent and hypnotic rhythm. Some without a drum pounded on pots, pans, tables, and chairs. Others simply clapped their hands and used every part of their bodies as instruments.

The old woman began to sing and soon the entire congregation joined in. Their song had no recognizable words, nor did it have a familiar melodic structure. Yet it spoke to Lakshmi on a cellular level. She understood the message. The villagers' song spoke of love and unity; spoke of connection to the earth, sky, moon and stars; to the rivers and the sea, to our animal brethren and to each other. The song of the Others proclaimed that there is no Other. Only One.

By the "time" the Others commenced to dancing, Lakshmi was overcome with their beauty, and tears rolled down her cheeks. Special Ed too, was moved to sing and howl along with them, for after all, their message of connection to all creatures certainly included Special Ed.

And the dancing! The villagers' legs were coiled metal springs which propelled them so high that their feet effortlessly cleared their companions' heads. With each vertical jump, they hung in slow motion before returning to earth, then bounced straight up again. All the while, these multi-colored human pogo sticks continued to beat their infectious rhythm, sing their primal song, and cast a rapturous communal gaze directly into Lakshmi's eyes.

It's mysterious, how rarely we remember our dreams—as if our thought molecules get swept into and absorbed by a raging river of thought molecules, never to be seen again. So, it is no surprise that Lakshmi had no conscious recollection of the singing and dancing elders who visited her on the Boat of Bob in Chapter One. However, something in the Others' ceremony felt rather familiar, and she could not help but feel she'd been here before.

*

After the reception, Lakshmi's thought molecules transported her inside a tent, still holding the old woman's hand.

"My name is Una," she began. "Sit down, my dear, while I tell you a story."

Una lowered herself to the ground and Lakshmi followed her lead. They sat facing each other with legs crossed so close that their knees touched. Lakshmi felt very small—no more than five years old. She remembered her Grandma Aanya: her breasts like big warm pillows when she held her close; her scent of lavender mixed with chai; the way she cocked her head slightly when she adored her with her smile. Mostly, Lakshmi remembered how safe she felt when she was held by Grandma Aanya.

"May I call you Grandma Una?" she asked. Her voice was very high—a child's voice emanating from a five-year-old's body.

"Why, of course you may," said Una, her face glowing radiant gold.

"Once upon a 'time,' " she began, "there were no Others. There was only One. We people were One with Earth, and Earth was One with us. The animals, forests, and seas lived intertwined in harmony, each part drawing nourishment from the whole, a grand orchestra with every instrument playing its part in the eternal symphony of life, death, and rebirth. Earth too, played its part, in harmony with her neighboring planets that revolved around the sun which pricked the sky along with a thousand million other suns in our galaxy, which joined its millions upon millions of brother and sister galaxies, and on and on."

Una's golden visage melded into sage, and she continued. "But one day, a man called Randayn became greedy. Randayn convinced his family that there wasn't enough food, shelter, or love to go around. He told them stories to make them very scared. He said greed was a virtue and generosity a sin. He taught his people to hate the Big Nosed Clan, for they were surely taking what rightfully belonged to the Randayn family and threatening their way of life."

Una's face turned scarlet. "Randayn taught his family that the Big-Nosed Clan was stupid and slothful. They were wretched, immoral, inhuman. They were Others."

Young Lakshmi leaned closer to Grandma Una. "This story is scaring me," she whimpered.

"Come here, little one. I'll hold you close, but it's a story you must hear."

Lakshmi crawled into Una's lap. Una held her close to her bosom, and with her face now a brilliant shade of violet, she continued.

"The Randayns were very cruel to the Big-Nosed Clan. They enslaved them and stole everything they had. This went on for decades, centuries even. But, as people will do, the Randayns and the Big-Nosed Clan interbred until you could no longer tell them apart."

"Then what happened?" asked little Lakshmi. "Did they become One again?"

"You would think so," was Una's reply, her face turning sky blue. "They did, in fact, become the Big-Nosed Randayns. They left each other in peace for a while until they saw that there were those among them whose ears were rather small.

"So the Big-Nosed Randayns declared the Big-Nosed-Small-Eared Randayns to be the Others. They rounded them up and imprisoned them in concentration camps. 'Re-education centers,' they called them. The Big-Nosed-Small-Eared Randayns suffered greatly for generations. But something odd happened."

"What was that, Grandma Una?"

"Well, child," she said as her face turned sepia, "a new breed of Big-Nosed-Small-Eared Randayns evolved. They possessed chocolate colored skin, and they became known as the Big-Nosed-Small-Eared-Brown-Skinned Randayns. The Big-Nosed-Small-Eared Randayns were so happy to have someone to call the Others that they kicked the Big-Nosed-Small-Eared-Brown-Skinned Randayns out of their homes, denied them food rations, and banished them to the most desolate reaches of our land.

"Our people's history has always told the same story. Those who are different are punished and called the Others. But as soon as the Others' numbers and power grow, they find a smaller, weaker group, and make them the Others. It's as predictable as rain."

"I don't like this story," said little Lakshmi.

"Hush, my child," said Una, her cheeks radiating crimson. "We are coming to the part that you must know. Let me tell you about MISTER BIGLY."

MISTER BIGLY... Lakshmi had heard that name somewhere before... She had a vague recollection of an upside-down couple—the Brains? Yes, Philbert and Hazel Brain! They stood on their heads in Chapter Two! It seemed to Lakshmi that maybe Mr. and Mrs. Brain had made mention of someone named MISTER BIGLY.

"When MISTER BIGLY came along, he declared all of us—red, blue, green, yellow, and brown—to be Others. He took away our right to work, to own homes, to even speak against him—and he cast us out to live in this 're-education center.' He ordered every one of us to be branded with an 'O' on our foreheads. Not only were we to be branded, he decreed that the animals, birds, trees, rivers, and oceans were Others, and they should be branded too. He even branded the Earth!

"He stood truth on its head," Una continued, her face now a beatific rainbow. "MISTER BIGLY claimed he was white-skinned, although any blind person could see he was orange. 'I'm the whitest person on the planet,' he told his Minions. 'Everybody knows that.'

"There was the 'time' MISTER BIGLY broke into Quick 'n' Easy Burger and made off with an entire moving van full of cheeseburgers. The surveillance cameras captured it all, but that didn't trouble MISTER BIGLY. First, he said, 'Of course I took them! Go watch the video of me passing them out to the hurricane victims on Other Island.'

Una went on. "Yes, there was a video of MISTER BIGLY at Other Island tossing something to the starving masses like a basketball player shooting free throws. Unfortunately, what he was tossing were used-up cheeseburger wrappers.

"When he returned home, he opened his empty moving van, belched, and said, 'Cheeseburgers? What cheeseburgers? You can see for yourself, there are no cheeseburgers in this truck. All those videos of me stealing cheeseburgers are bogus news. Bogus News!' Then he belched again.

"This led to the crisis known as the Great Cheeseburger Shortage. Overnight, our nation's entire cheeseburger supply mysteriously disappeared. The Others suspected MISTER BIGLY, but he vehemently denied his guilt and called it 'Bogus News.' Then he sent his upside-down Minions to round up thousands of Others and had them summarily executed for the crime of Grand Theft Cheeseburger. It was terrible!

"Just a year later, the World Book of Records, after carefully studying the incident, declared MISTER BIGLY the all-'time' champion for most cheeseburgers eaten in a 24-hour period. Now it's something you will often hear him brag about."

"I hope I never hear him brag about that or anything else," declared little Lakshmi.

"Oh, I'm afraid you will, my dear. And when you do, you must be very careful not to stand on your head."

"I won't, Grandma Una," she said, recalling Hazel and Philbert Brain and the upside-down pipers.

"MISTER BIGLY has stood the truth on its head, and he has ordered his Minions to stand on their heads too. 'BIGLY's Minions,' he calls them, or BMs for short. MISTER BIGLY brags that his BMs love him so much, he can do anything and they will love him for it.

"It's one of the few things MISTER BIGLY has said that's true. Once, MISTER BIGLY walked out onto Main Street at high noon and shot a man dead, right in front of God and a hundred Minions. Can you guess what happened, dear?"

"Did they call the police? Did they arrest him?"

Lakshmi's thought molecules drifted away from the tent and into the scene of MISTER BIGLY's heinous crime. There stood MISTER BIGLY holding the smoking gun, a man lying dead on the ground with a bullet in his brain, while the BMs, standing on their heads, gathered 'round.

"Great shot, MISTER BIGLY!" cried one.

"He must have deserved it," declared another.

"It's a free country! We demand the right to kill anybody who would deny us our right to kill him!" reasoned another.

Then, five-year-old Lakshmi was back in the tent with Grandma Una.

"You see," said Grandma Una, stroking Lakshmi's hair, "MISTER BIGLY has turned his Minions on their heads, and his upside-down world is spreading like a terrible disease. Why, just last week I saw some of our blue people standing on their heads, and they were ganging up on the red people

86

and burning their tents. Even the yellows, of all people, are beginning to do headstands and bully the greens!

"If we don't stop MISTER BIGLY, before long he will have all of humanity standing on its head and fighting over who can best turn the truth upside-down. His BMs say they're cutting down trees to save the forests. They say they're ridding the planet of poisonous carbon by releasing it into the air. They're buying assault weapons to prevent gun violence. They're building nuclear weapons to prevent war. They're..."

A rustling sound came from the tent opening. Ducking his head in from the outside entered the most handsome young man in the history of handsome young men. His complexion was creamy mocha, his shoulder-length hair flowing raven-black. Unlike his ragged compatriots, his attire was that of an elegant prince, what with the white cotton blouse wide open at the neck, the dashing black waistcoat with the upturned collar, the perfectly fitting tan trousers, the wide pirate's belt matching the boots of Spanish leather. But, however dazzling his finery, it only served to accentuate the Adonis-like body that rippled beneath the surface of his garb.

Most striking of all were the young man's eyes. The color of dark chocolate, they penetrated the object of his attention's soul with love, compassion, and a deep knowing beyond his years. At this moment, the object of his attention was Lakshmi.

"Oh Lance," said Una. "I'm so happy to see you! Lakshmi, this is my grandson, Lance Lovesalot."

"So wonderful to meet you, Lakshmi," said the prince in a thrillingly mellifluous voice. He smiled benevolently and held out two regal hands.

"Oh my," said Lakshmi, no longer a 5-year-old girl, but very much a 20-year-old young woman.

Lance Lovesalot

11. LOVE STORY

A disclaimer from the author regarding
his motives for the chapter's subject
matter; Lance Lovesalot performs an
elaborate mating ritual; Lakshmi and Lance
consummate their love in an unusual manner
that is graphically described.

DEAR READER, in the art of contemporary storytelling,
whether the account be fact or fiction, whether the tale
be delivered through literature, poetry, stage, or screen,
it is common knowledge that, in order for a work to be
commercially viable, for it to survive the gauntlet posed by
the cutthroat communication industries—and in the current
context of our disposable society, for a story to hold an
impatient public's attention longer than it takes to change
the channel, it is imperative that the narrative prominently
features a compelling love interest.

In the case of the fable at hand, this author is well aware
that no amount of profound philosophizing, rapturous
soliloquizing, sensational indulgence, or subtle lyricism—no
flights of fancy such as people changing colors or standing
on their heads—not even an element as compelling as a
talking dog—will capture the reader's attention like two
people entwined in a good, juicy love story.

Further, it is not sufficient to simply explore the emotional dynamics between two individuals as they grapple with the complexities of intimate bonding. No, in today's world, with our faculties relentlessly stupefied by sensory overload, there is only one method to ensure that the storyteller will score with the public, in a manner of speaking. Only one formula is tried, true, and guaranteed to hold the audience's rapt attention regardless of the credibility of the story or the skill with which it is delivered. The mechanism in question will be employed liberally in this chapter. It is a device known as: "Gratuitous Sex."

Courtship

"Come," he said.

Lakshmi took his outstretched hands in hers, and together they exited the tent. Lance Lovesalot led her to an ancient oak where he lifted her effortlessly and sat her on a sturdy branch five feet above the ground. From her perch, she observed with a cryptic mix of intoxicated interest and feigned boredom. The mating dance began.

Lance's opening gambit involved much stalking and stomping while his eyes locked with hers, as if the courting couple were engaged in pitched battle. He plodded slowly in a semi-circle like a sumo wrestler around Lakshmi's roost, dragging his left foot and stomping emphatically with his right, then reversing the order. Each stomp increased in force and proximity as Lance methodically closed the circle. When he arrived just inches from where Lakshmi sat, he stomped with his left, stomped with his right, leaped high above her head and landed vehemently, crouching before her on the ground.

Lakshmi yawned.

Undeterred, Lance employed the "time"-tested Cape of Many Colors Maneuver. Slung around his neck was a black cloak which he pulled over his head so only his eyes peaked out. Then, with sudden drama, he threw back the cloak and bat-like, he spread it open above his head, revealing a regal array of magenta, cerulean, and gold.

Lakshmi stifled a gasp, then glanced distractedly over her shoulder as if to say, "This is mildly interesting. I wonder if there's something better over that hill…"

She busily filed her nails.

A guitar materialized in Lance's hands and he began to play a progression of chords, each one more exquisite than the last. With every downward strum, he leaned in smiling toward Lakshmi as if to offer her the gift of a chord. Humming seductively, he gazed deeply into her eyes.

She dropped her nail file.

Lance abruptly stopped his humming, and thereupon he parted his lips to sing. Out came the most melodious, honey-drenched, soulful voice Lakshmi had ever heard. The song he sang spoke of "time" and rivers, mountains and valleys, earth and fire, and souls entwined in eternal love.

Lakshmi found herself reluctantly humming along, then tentatively joining in on the chorus. Before she knew, she and Lance had burst into an elaborate operatic duet—Lakshmi singing soprano, Lance in his rich baritone—the two of them arm-in-arm, cheek-to-cheek, gazing plaintively toward the heavens.

The song ended with their voices holding the final exquisite note in a perfectly synchronized vibrato. With their faces separated by mere inches, silence tentatively dangled while their last note floated pregnant in the air. Lance leaned in for the kiss; however, Lakshmi demurely turned away. The deal was not yet closed.

First, custom demanded that Lance build Lakshmi a house. Lest the reader need reminding, the "time"/space continuum we encounter in a dream is a foreign concept to our waking consciousness. Hence, Lakshmi's thought molecules created a scenario in which, one moment Lance was chain sawing enormous firs, hauling them over his shoulder to the building site, and hammering in some boards. The next moment, the log cabin was built. By conventional standards, it could be said that Lance's structure went up rather fast.

With the cabin now proudly standing, there was but one thing left to do. Lance swooped Lakshmi into his arms and, as they joined in a tender reprise of their vocal duet, he carried her across the threshold into their love nest.

Consummation

Swirling in the endorphin-drenched romance that engulfed Lakshmi's senses were thought molecules that brought to the forefront a book Lakshmi had enjoyed as a child—an interactive publication, if you will, which had provided many hours of creative, thought-provoking entertainment for Lakshmi and her friends in their formative years. This book which now played a prominent role in the Lance/Lakshmi liaison was entitled Mad Libs.

Mad Libs provided story lines in which key words or phrases were left empty, with the reader inviting a second participant to fill in the blanks. Adding to the intrigue, the player was instructed to choose a designated part of speech without seeing the sentence that was being completed. For example, the first sentence describing Lance and Lakshmi's lovemaking took shape in Lakshmi's thought molecules thusly:

Lakshmi and Lance tumbled into the _____ in a writhing
$\qquad$ furniture item

tangle of _____.
$\qquad$ emotion

The words Lakshmi blindly chose to fill in were: bathtub and histrionics. So, it followed that the sentence in question read:

Lakshmi and Lance tumbled into the **bathtub** in a writhing
$\qquad$ furniture item

tangle of **histrionics**.

emotion

We will intercept Lakshmi's thought molecules from that point and see where they lead. The audience should be forewarned that the following descriptions may be graphic and unsuitable for those with more delicate sensibilities.

Lakshmi and Lance tumbled into the **bathtub** in a writhing

furniture item

tangle of **histrionics**. Lance breathlessly ripped off her

emotion

glasses while Lakshmi **obsessively** licked his **nose**. "**Ouch!**"

clothing item   adverb   body part exclamation

exclaimed Lakshmi, as Lance reached into her **shoes** and

clothing item

fondled her **big toe**. "My, how **insignificant** you are," she

body part   adjective

panted, as she stroked his throbbing **elbow**. "I don't know

body part

how I'll ever manage to **inflate** that. "Don't worry," said

verb

Lance, "I'll be **creative**." Deftly as a **lug wrench**, Lance

adjective   noun

slid his **thumb** into Lakshmi's **eye** as she moaned with

body part   body part

confusion. "Oh, Lance!" she cried, "what **ridiculous back**

emotion   adjective body part

hair you have!" "All the better to **shock** you with," replied

                            verb

Lance. Now, all **hygiene** was abandoned. The couple

descriptive noun

gobbled each other with breathless **idiosyncrasy** until

past tense verb   adjective

all that remained were their **quirky** rhythms and their

adjective

contrapuntal cries. Simultaneously, the two reached the

adjective

apex of their **scrum**. With an explosion of **helium**, every

active noun   noun

balloon was released.

noun

Aftermath

It was over. Lance and Lakshmi had performed the ancient dance of procreation and Lance had successfully planted his seed. Equally important, he had satisfied the prurient interest of the reader. Hence, like the praying mantis that was metaphorically referenced in the previous chapter, his job was finished. And no, Lakshmi did not bite off Lance's head in accordance with the ritual of the female mantis. She simply dismissed him with her thought molecules and Lance Lovesalot disappeared into the ether.

Lakshmi lay satiated in the bathtub of the aforementioned Mad Libs exercise, rubbing her belly and communing with the new, microscopic life that grew inside her. But then an ominous thought crossed her mind: "Where's Special Ed?"

"Special Ed quietly exited the tent."

12. SPECIAL ED'S ADVENTURE

Special Ed lights out on his own: a meditation on dog nature ensues; Special Ed discovers some young playmates; receives an education and entreaty from a pack of wolves; is named to an ambassadorship.

WHEN UNA BEGAN telling Lakshmi about the Others while they sat in the tent, Special Ed sashayed up to Lakshmi and enjoyed her petting for a while. When Lakshmi's hand seemed to lose interest, he rambled over to Una and plopped his head in her lap. Una did a lovely job with the ears, and when Special Ed lifted his head, she scratched the chin rather nicely. But while he knew all this talk about the Others was most assuredly important, it seemed a bit abstract for his taste. He would much prefer to be outdoors, seeing new sights, sniffing new smells, meeting new beings, and gulping up a heaping helping of the world. So, he quietly exited the tent.

Once outside, Special Ed scurried out into the big open air, nose sweeping the ground, registering news of all the recent events. There was much to catch up on. A pregnant rabbit passed this way not more than an hour ago. Some sort of big bird—an owl(?)—was hot on her trail. There were moles hiding somewhere underground. It rained last week. Dead leaves lay in his path smelling like it was going to be a cold winter.

Special Ed loved people and he loved Lakshmi more than anybody, but truth be told, he felt happy to take a break from humans. Although he was quite fluent in Lakshmi's English, it was still a second language for him and much easier to converse in his own. If he'd thought it through, it might have dawned on him that no matter how hard he worked to understand people's language, they didn't try very hard to understand his.

Take barking for example. Most humans thought when a dog barked, he was just yelling his fool head off. They couldn't even distinguish between the most basic barks like "Welcome," and "I'm protecting my home," and "I'm so happy to see you." They didn't know the difference between a German Shepherd saying, "I am boss here and I expect obedience and order," and a Chihuahua announcing, "I'm a neurotic little imbecile with a pea-brain and I will shout it to the heavens!" (More on this shortly.)

Sometimes it was better to take a holiday from humans and just be a dog. Humans bothered their brains with so much to think about: He said...She said...What's going to happen next year?...I must build a better machine...What is the meaning of existence?...and the Others...and MISTER BIGLY...and.... It was all so complicated!

Special Ed needed a vacation from all that. He needed to simply live for a while—see the sights, smell the news, run through the tall grass, roll in the dirt. Pee on trees, poop on the ground, kick up his scent with his back legs to tell everybody Special Ed was here.

He'd get back to his job of teaching humans in a little while. It was demanding work. Those poor people—there was so much they didn't understand. "Stop and smell the roses," they said. But they hardly ever did. Special Ed constantly had to remind them.

Humans liked to say, "Be here now." But they were always watching TV or tapping their phone or blabbing about any old thing that came to their mind. Every day, Special Ed tried to teach them the three most basic concepts: Be, Be Here, and Be Here Now.

Humans always talked about "unconditional love." Then they broke up into teams and fought wars over whose love was better. Even people on the same team didn't seem to love each other all that much. Special Ed was gifted at unconditional love, and he hoped someday his beloved humans would get the hang of it too.

With his tongue hanging out the side of his smiling mouth and his tail sweeping high and wide, he trotted over to an old cedar tree and sniffed the trunk. Observing that a small dog had recently peed on the tree, Special Ed deemed it important to announce his presence. He lifted his leg to pee in the same direction, mindful to aim higher than the previous visitor, thereby establishing for the record that a larger, more substantial dog had claimed the territory.

Not that Special Ed was convinced that the creature whose pee he was overriding was, in fact, a dog. "Possibly a Chihuahua," thought Special Ed. "Or maybe Dachshund." From the slightly bitter quality of the bouquet, it might have been a Pomeranian. But most assuredly not a dog.

Not that Special Ed held a negative judgment toward the above-mentioned creatures. On the contrary, he entertained no animosity toward any living being. Rather than seeing them as Others, he understood we are all equal parts that add up to the whole in this big wide world.

Special Ed felt no ill-will toward those snarling little creatures who yap incessantly at every real or imagined object that occupies space in their tiny brains; who bite at the heels of every human who dares to intrude on their sheltered space; who pick a fight with every Great Dane they meet because what else does one do when one is scared of another who is ten "times" one's size?

No, he bore no grudge against Chihuahuas, Dachshunds, Pomeranians, and the like. But simply put, those animals did not resemble anything Special Ed had ever encountered that he knew to be a "dog."

*

Meandering on the outskirts of the Others' encampment, Special Ed came across a group of children absorbed in a game that involved kicking a partially deflated ball. If Special Ed had been able to discern colors, he would have seen the beautiful array of purple, green, and orange variations in the children's skin tones. But although Special Ed's color sense was somewhat limited, he compensated with his soul sense, which was remarkably acute.

"Oh boy!" cried Special Ed, and into the fray he charged, swooping up the ball in his mouth and prancing away. Like a football running back, he zigged, he zagged, he juked and head faked, changing directions on a dime, all the while ten grubby, laughing children chased him to no avail. They tried to corral him, but Special Ed was too fast and clever. He eluded every would-be tackler, and soon he broke into the open field where he threatened to abscond forever with his opponents' ball. But to their surprise, the moment he was free, he skidded to a stop. He dropped his prize and stood panting before it, gazing happily into the youngster's eyes.

"Throw me the ball!" he barked. "Throw me the ball!"

The largest of the group stepped forward and scooped up the ball. He faked a throw and Special Ed, not understanding the concept of a "lie," went sprinting off in pursuit of the phantom throw. After thirty yards or so, he stopped, looked around, and discovered the kid still had the ball which he threw in the opposite direction. Special Ed raced after it and swooped it up, never breaking his stride. The children laughed and cheered. Then he dropped it where he stood. Panting and drooling, he barked, "Throw me the ball!"

Rather than the author copy/pasting the above event multiple "times," suffice to say that very scenario played out over and over and over.

But all good things must come to an end. Special Ed became so winded his eyes were popping out of his head and his tongue was falling out of his mouth. He wished they would stop throwing the ball so he wouldn't have to keep chasing it. Eventually, his wish was granted as, one by one, the children became bored and peeled away.

*

In the aftermath of the merriment, Special Ed found himself most assuredly thirsty. He stuck his nose in the air and sniffed. Sifting through a potpourri of aromas—apple trees shedding their overripe fruit, earthworms crawling underground, a raccoon nearby, humans in the distance—he was able to discern running water in the vicinity. He trotted toward the scent and shortly, his ears verified what his nose had already ascertained. Then his eyes found it too: a cold, inviting river.

Special Ed stepped gingerly with his forepaws into the water's edge and feasted on the fresh water to his heart's content. Growing braver, he moseyed in with all four paws and lapped up some more. Gradually, he waded in until his stomach was submerged. "Time" to take a swim. He caught the gentle current and allowed it to carry him where it would.

Puzzling, thought Special Ed, what a fuss humans make of such things. The moment water touches them, they scream and squeal and complain about how freezing it is. The little ones sink and need adults to hold them up while they flail around. Special Ed would never have given all these water issues a second thought if he hadn't seen it for himself. You get in, you swim. Freezing water gives you energy, makes you happy and alive. What else is there to know?

"Everything is so complicated with these poor humans," Special Ed thought. "If only they were smart enough to understand how simple life is."

*

Back on the bank, Special Ed gave himself a good shake from head to tail. He missed Lakshmi. If she were here, he'd shake right in front of her so he could share some of the river with her.

Still wet, Special Ed rolled on the grassy bank to dry himself some more. He might have rolled even if he had been dry, for his back was itching and in need of a good scratch. Sliding along the ground, belly absorbing the sun, paws reaching for the trees, Special Ed smelled something familiar yet foreign. Dogs? Not precisely. More like...

Wolves. Two couples. Initially, Special Ed only recognized their scent from the pack that had greeted him at the Others' camp. But as they murmured to each other, he was able to identify each distinctive voice he had heard upon his first encounter. Then he saw the familiar O's burned into their foreheads.

He thought it best to remain splayed on his back as the wolves circled him and sniffed his orifices. They approached guardedly with one of the females nervously hopping back at each sudden movement. Upon completing their inspection, the most regal of the pack rendered judgment.

"We mean you no harm," he declared.

With that, Special Ed sprang to his feet, and another round of nudging, poking, smelling, and testing commenced. This "time," Special Ed joined in. Along with learning each other's age, health status, and what they had eaten that day, they also determined each other's strengths, weaknesses, fears, and intelligence. Thus, at the conclusion of this introduction ceremony, he and the wolves knew each other quite well.

"Listen," said the leader. "There are some important things you must understand."

Special Ed perked up his ears. He recognized that these were older, wiser, more intelligent beings than he, therefore they must be afforded proper esteem.

"You, Special Ed," continued the leader, "have been assigned an essential task. You are our official Wildlife Ambassador."

"Me?" he asked.

"Yes. You see, you are the bridge we need to help humans understand us. You're fluent enough in their language, so you're uniquely qualified to translate for us."

"I'm confused," said Special Ed.

"Let me explain," said the elder. "Long ago, some of our predecessors befriended humans. They figured out that if they hung around the campfire and made themselves adorable, the humans would feed them scraps.

"These ancestors lived by the motto: 'Survival of the Friendliest.' They learned to melt their humans' hearts by looking lovingly into their eyes—just like a baby does with its mother. And sure enough, the people would say, 'Aaah… Isn't he cute?!'

"Your early forefathers and mothers decided to abandon their packs and cast their lot with their new human packs. They made the calculation that rather than running around with a pack of wolves trying to chase down a caribou, life would be cushier hanging around the campfire begging humans to throw them a bone."

"I like hanging around my people and begging," offered Special Ed. "I can sit real straight and show them my big brown eyes and make myself look very charming."

"I know you can," said the wolf. "And your people love you for that. Over generations and centuries, they bred you to be just as you are: docile, friendly, and lovable. They thought our pointy ears looked scary, so they even bred some of you to have floppy ears."

"I have floppy ears," ventured Special Ed. "Don't I look scary?"

All four wolves burst into hearty laughter. Then they pounced on him in a chaos of snarls, growls, and bristled fur. They pinned him to the ground while the leader closed his frothing mouth around Special Ed's neck. The wolf's sharp teeth glistened as they clamped onto Special Ed's jugular, but they did not sink in. On a cue imperceptible to humans, the four wolves stepped back simultaneously, leaving Special Ed to remain on his back, wide-eyed, tail between his legs, heart racing, wolf foam glistening on his throat.

"No, you don't look scary," said the Alpha. "Get up."

Special Ed obeyed and the wolf continued. "We look scary. We look scary to humans because we're wild. We scare them because we remind them of what they used to be and pretend not to be. They say we're killers which is, by the way, what every animal on this planet happens to be: a killer."

"Humans calling us killers," piped in the leader's mate, "is like a skunk saying a rabbit stinks."

"It's like a parrot saying a rhinoceros talks too much," said the second male.

"It's like a dog saying a wolf is stupid," chimed in his mate.

"We're not stupid, are we?" asked the leader.

"No sir. Most assuredly not," said Special Ed.

"Correct. Now, where were we? Oh, right—we're so scary they want to kill us. Why, just yesterday, MISTER BIGLY's sons, Rufus and Doofus, buzzed us in their helicopters and shot at our pack. We got lucky. Rufus missed and shot Doofus's ear off, so they had to call it a day.

"But it's not just us. MISTER BIGLY has designated all wild animals as "Others," and his Minions are trying to exterminate every one of us.

"Our wild animal numbers are dwindling. People keep coming and coming, stealing our land, laying down concrete, building new settlements, flushing us out. That's where you come in," said the leader's mate.

"Me?" asked Special Ed. He couldn't imagine why.

"Yes, you," Alpha Male replied. "As I said, you speak people's language. You remind humans of their wild selves that they forgot so long ago. But you do it so kindly and politely that they love you for it.

"You show them that we're all connected to earth, sky, water, trees, and each other. You help them remember how to be animals again. You teach them that there is only this moment and no other. Through you, humans may come to realize that in destroying us, they're destroying you—they're destroying themselves."

"You're the only one who can do this," said the leader's mate. "We're too wild, too frightening. They don't understand us. But you, they understand."

Back to the Alpha: "Return to your humans, Special Ed. Teach them that we wild things are not 'Others.' Show them that we're all a part of each other, that we're all in this together. Teach them to love us the way they love you, the way they love their own."

"You are our liaison, Special Ed," the four wolves cried in unison. "We hereby name you Wildlife Ambassador. Go forth and represent us. Be on your way and make peace."

And with that, Wildlife Ambassador Special Ed bid fond farewell to his wolf ancestors, the music of their howls still ringing in his ears.

*

Back in Lakshmi and Lance's love nest, Lakshmi soon discovered the answer to her question: "Where's Special Ed?" Seems he'd been sleeping under the bed during the entire romantic ruckus.

It's a peculiar characteristic among dogs: They become excited when people display the slightest hint of enthusiasm. Yet, when confronted with human lovemaking, regardless the volume or degree of athleticism, they're lulled into contented sleep like a baby being rocked in the cradle. Such was the case with Special Ed who, during Lakshmi and Lance's frolic, had curled up under the bed and fallen into a deep slumber, the aphrodisiac overhead performing as a sedative below.

Which begs the question: Did Special Ed really participate in this chapter's adventure or was it a dream? And if it was the latter, whose dream was it? As it appears that Special Ed is a product of Lakshmi's dream, the logical conclusion would be that her thought molecules created the above scenario.

However, as has been noted, Lakshmi was rather preoccupied during the "time" Special Ed was on the loose. So, was it Special Ed's dream? One could make the case that Lakshmi and Special Ed's thought molecules were so entwined that Special Ed may have had a dream within Lakshmi's dream.

Then again, it could be argued that this story is entirely a figment of the author's imagination, in which case, isn't it the author's responsibility to determine where this dream originated? Could it be that it was the author's dream? At which point, the author must offer the caveat that these questions are vastly beyond his expertise, imagination, and frankly, his interest. So, suffice to say, it happened. The veracity of this event is affirmed by the fact that the words appear on these very pages, and therefore, the author has declared it "Good."

Row, row, row your boat.

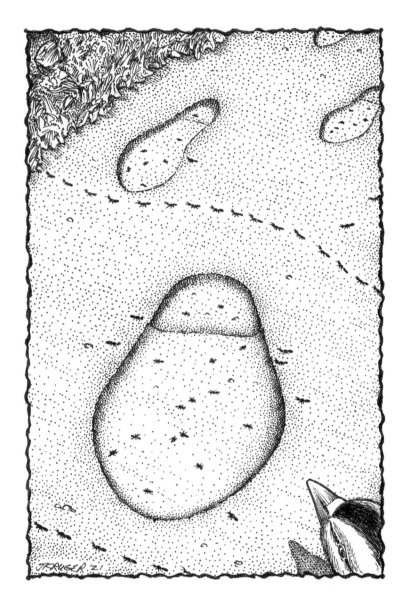

"Forgive me, poor ants. I meant you no harm."

13. UNINTENDED CONSEQUENCES

The two wanderers embark on a most unusual trail: encounter an equally unusual man who regales them with a cautionary tale describing a disturbing sequence of events; culminating in a desperate escape from the forest in the midst of an animal stampede.

THE NEXT MORNING, a satiated Lakshmi and newly appointed Ambassador Special Ed stirred with the morning sunlight that streamed through the cabin window. Lakshmi's thought molecules had vaporized Lance Lovesalot, leaving a vacancy in the bed which Special Ed saw fit to occupy halfway through the night. Upon waking, Lakshmi found herself precariously positioned on the bed's precipice as Special Ed leaned the totality of his body into hers. He must have been dreaming of chasing a squirrel or some such thing, for all four paws were running in place, knocking the covers askew and jostling Lakshmi out of her post-coital slumber. He let out little yips as he thumped his tail from side to side like a pendulum, further adding to the mayhem. Lakshmi might have overlooked Special Ed's nocturnal exuberances, but they were accompanied by the most malodorous emissions that, while potentially pleasing to another dog, she found decidedly unattractive. "Time" to get up.

In a dream, there is no need to attend to such details as eating, dressing, or morning constitution. Even coffee might be considered expendable. Consequently, Lakshmi's thought molecules delivered her and Special Ed directly from the bed on which they had slept to the open cabin door. They walked outside.

With her first step, Lakshmi alighted upon a dusty trail that began at the cabin's doorstep and meandered far into a deep wood. Feeling compelled to see where it led, she embarked on the trail with Special Ed trotting by her side while curiously sniffing the ground.

They hadn't gone far when she turned to take one last look at the cabin. To her dismay, the fire she and Lance had built in the stone fireplace was still burning and sending black plumes of smoke out the chimney. Lakshmi watched in horror as swallows fell choking from the sky. It seems they had built a nest in the flue and now they were getting smoked out.

"Oh my!" cried Lakshmi. "I never would have made a fire had I known I was destroying their home!"

They walked on a bit farther and once again Lakshmi looked back. Although the trail was dry, she was surprised to see that every step she and Special Ed had taken left deep, wide footprints. Buried in each of those footprints were scores of ants, crushed beneath the travelers' feet, some belly up and flailing for life, others flattened and dead.

"Oh dear," Lakshmi sighed. "Forgive me, poor ants. I meant you no harm."

As they followed the trail to the wooded entrance, they chanced upon a sign, much as one would find at a park trailhead. It read:

YE OLDE UNINTENDED CONSEQUENCES TRAIL

"Let's make a go, Lakshmi," said Special Ed.

"I didn't expect this," she said.

"We're here because we're here. Let's make a go!"

"Okay, Special Ed. What do we have to lose? Let's make a go!"

*

Entering the woods, the trees stretched so tall they blocked the sun. So thick and packed together were the giant conifers that the only way through them was the narrow trail on which our two protagonists walked. They hadn't gone far when Lakshmi announced, "I wish I knew where we were going."

With that, they came upon a second sign, a wooden board sloppily nailed to a tree. The scruffy handwritten message said:

"Be careful what you wish for."

"Maybe we should turn around," declared Lakshmi. But as she looked behind her, she saw that a fortress of trees had sprung up where the path had been, blocking their only way out.

"Well now," she said. "*That's* interesting."

"Look," barked Special Ed. "Another sign!"

They walked a little faster until the weather-beaten board came into sharp relief. The crude lettering read:

Ancient Chinese curse: May you live in interesting "times."

"Interesting indeed," said Lakshmi. "I didn't plan on *this*."

They walked a short distance further when they spotted yet another sign:

"Life is what happens to you while you're busy making other plans."

—John Lennon

There was no turning around. With each step, the trees encroached upon the trail they had previously traversed, leaving only one option: Keep moving forward.

"I don't know where we're heading," said Lakshmi, "but at least we're going *somewhere*."

"Ya can't stop progress," offered Special Ed.

Just then, a sign popped up out of the ground directly in front of them. This one read:

"Is it progress if a cannibal uses a fork?"

—Stanislaw Jerzy Lec

*

If we measure progress, not by cannibals using forks but by distance covered, it could be said that Lakshmi and Special Ed made much progress on Ye Olde Unintended Consequences Trail. However, the more miles they traveled, the more conditions remained the same, what with the impenetrable forest on either side and the encroaching trees springing up in the hikers' wake. They trudged on.

After many miles and an undetermined amount of "time," the monotony of their journey was disrupted by a raucous tumult in the forest. Off to their right, they heard a bedlam of thrashing, crashing, thudding, crunching, muttering, sputtering, growling, and howling. Lakshmi would have mistaken the turmoil to be emanating from a wild boar but for the cursing in the Queen's English which gave the confusion a decidedly human ambience.

Lakshmi's intuitions were confirmed when, out of the woods and directly before them staggered a most disheveled and discombobulated member of the Homo Erectus species. He appeared to be sprouting twigs and branches which clung tenaciously to his tattered tweed coat. His face and hands were criss-crossed with scratches he'd suffered in the course of battle with the forest guardians. He bent down to pick up his battered ball cap which lay kayoed on the ground. Dusting it off, he replaced it over his Einstein-white hair. The cap read: "What Could Go Wrong?"

"Oh me and it's oh my and it's oh me again," he fussed. "This will never do. Never do, I predict. Never ever do at all."

Lakshmi observed the spectacle open-mouthed, while Special Ed, speaking in his native tongue, shouted, "Halt! Who goes there?"

"Oh boy and it's oh man and it's oh boy again," soliloquized the man, brushing fir needles from his mud-stained trousers. "I already know who *I* am. But the question is: Who are *you*? Wait, wait. Don't say a word. If you do, you might set off a chain of events that could destroy the world. Oh well. All right. Okay. Go ahead and tell me. What could go wrong?"

"My name is Lakshmi Jackson," she said. "This is my friend, Special Ed. We've been looking for the River of Truth. But we seem to have lost our way. And, by the way, who are *you*?"

"Me? Oh dear and it's oy vey! How rude of me. At the risk of instigating a catastrophe of unintended consequences, allow me to introduce myself. My name is Rodney Fumblunder."

"Nice to meet you Mr. Flumbunder. We were…"

"Not *Flumb*under! *Fumblunder*!" he exploded. "You see? I told you my name and you messed it up. It's the unintended consequences of having a name like Fumblunder. No one ever gets it right."

"I'm so sorry, Mr. Flum…err…Fumblunder."

"The River of Truth, is it?" Fumblunder continued. "Truth is, we have to get out of these woods fast!"

"But why?"

"Because I tied my shoes this morning."

"Tied your shoes? But, what..."

"That's correct. I tied them in the double fisherman's knot, which everyone knows is impossible to untie."

"And that's why we have to get out of the woods?"

"Yes oh yes. Precisely. Affirmative."

"I'm afraid I don't understand, Mr. Flembinder."

"*Fumblunder*! You say *you* don't understand? How do you think *I* feel? I was just minding my own business this morning, tying my shoes in a double fisherman's knot. I went for a walk in the woods and when I came home, I began to take off my shoes. My wife Agnes insists I take my shoes off in the house."

"Agatha Fenderbender?"

"*Agnes Fumblunder*! Mrs. Fumblunder told me to take off my shoes. You can imagine what a conundrum this presented. As we all know, no one has ever untied the double fisherman's knot. However, I confronted the challenge by applying my deep scientific knowledge of principles and applications, and before long I achieved what no man has ever achieved."

"You untied the fisherman's knot in your shoes?"

"Yes yes and it's oh yes. Indeed I did. But as I set foot, if you will, where no man has ever trod, the unexpected happened."

"Unintended consequences?"

"Emphatically, yes. You see, as I set forth to solve the mystery of the double fisherman's knot, unraveling one by one the complex array of tangles that compose the eternal puzzle, I finally arrived at the final knot. After a lengthy amount of 'time' during which I wrestled the knot every which way, I finally felt a slackening, at which point I gave one mighty pull and the knot released. Unfortunately, in so doing, my hand flung backwards and struck the cat who, in turn, leaped out of the way and knocked over a kerosene lamp. The lamp fell against the window, setting the curtains aflame. Pretty soon, the entire cabin was on fire."

"Oh dear," exclaimed Lakshmi. "That's terrible!"

"Yes it was. All the more terrible because it caused Agnes to leave and spend some 'time' with her sister. Seems she didn't recognize my brilliance in untangling the double fisherman's knot. Another unintended consequence." He sighed.

"I'm sorry, Mr. Finbanger."

"*Fumblunder*! But as things will happen, it was for the best that Agnes left when she did. Because when I pulled out my trusty leaf blower to blow out the fire, I fanned the flames. The next thing I knew, these very woods were burning!"

"We'd better get out of here, Mr. Funglebungle," cried Lakshmi, "before the fire spreads this way!"

"*Fumblunder*! No, no. That's a negative," he declared. "The firemen came and put out the fire."

"Thank goodness," said Lakshmi.

"But," he continued, "when the crew dropped flame retardants from their helicopters, the toxins poisoned the animals, leaving the hearty ones choking for air, and their more fragile compatriots belly-up."

"Look," cried Special Ed. "Here they come now!"

Out of the woods they staggered: bears, boars, wolves, deer, squirrels, chipmunks, rabbits, raccoons, badgers, bobcat, moose, skunks, snakes, and frogs—flushed from the forest and choked by the red plume of smoke that the hovering helicopters poured down upon them like raining blood.

"Give us a stop!" coughed Special Ed. "We can't breathe!"

Peering down upon the bedlam were white men in black suits, black fedoras, black sunglasses, standing on their perches in their black helicopters, monitoring the carnage behind black binoculars. They neither smiled nor frowned nor cared. Down came the bright red chemicals.

Lakshmi and Rodney Fumblunder joined the animal exodus down Ye Olde Unintended Consequences Trail, while Special Ed ran ahead, behind, and alongside the choking parade, employing his herding skills to urge the fugitives onward.

"Head 'em up! Move 'em out!" he implored the stumbling animals as they lurched breathlessly forward. Special Ed stopped to grab a fallen fawn by the scruff of her neck, lifting her to her feet and nudging her ahead.

"There you go, dear deer," he said. "You can do it. C'mon everybody! Let's make a go!"

Hacking and tripping over lifeless bodies, Fumblunder dithered. "Oh gosh and it's oh gee! This is all because I tied my shoes in the double fisherman's knot. I have to fix this!"

"But how?" wheezed Lakshmi.

"There's a formula for this. Let's see. How does it go? Oh right! I think I remember. It goes something like this: 'When you're stuck in a rut, keep digging.' "

"I'm not sure that's how…"

"Oh yes and yes. It's affirmative. I'm sure of this now," he said.

And with that, Lakshmi's thought molecules put a shovel in Fumblunder's hands, and he commenced to digging a hole, right in the middle of Ye Olde Unintended Consequences Trail.

Lakshmi, Special Ed, and the surviving forest animals did not have the luxury of "time" to wait. They raced to escape the forest before they would smother and die. Overhead helicopters morphed into enormous midnight-colored wasps, their merciless eyes like black and blind footballs, their talons like those of a huge hawk. They swooped low and doused the fugitives with their toxic spray, causing the migration to stampede. Lakshmi saw a helicopter-sized wasp scoop up a cow and carry it away.

As she was swept into the tide, Lakshmi turned to take one last look behind her. There she saw Fumblunder, up to his neck in the hole and still digging. The last words she heard Rodney Fumblunder say were: "All because I tied my shoes in the double fisherman's knot!"

Down the trail, Rodney Fumblunder was gone. Wasps and helicopters gone. White men in black suits gone. Chemical cloud dissipated. Animals, those who'd survived, had peeled off into the forest, hoping to salvage what remained for them. This left Lakshmi and Special Ed trudging down the trail and arriving at a clearing. Off in the distance appeared a structure which, upon closer proximity, they determined to be a house.

A large, 3-story, dilapidated house it was: Roof shingles worn and askew; front porch sagging and railings unhinged; windows broken; pale blue peeling paint exposing large patches of naked wood, rotten and unattended. As Lakshmi and Special Ed approached, they read the sign in front that announced:

METAPHOR HOTEL

Lakshmi and Special Ed arrive at an unconventional hotel.

14. METAPHOR HOTEL

Lakshmi and Special Ed arrive at a thematic hotel; a conversation is sparked among an assortment of classic art icons; distinctions are drawn between literal and figurative interpretation; the Garden of Eden fable is reconstructed from the perspective of Adam, Eve, and the snake.

LAKSHMI PUSHED OPEN the front door and Special Ed followed her into the lobby. She noted the round tables, straight back chairs, and spittoons on the aged plank floor. The floral pattern on the faded yellow wall paper stood in sharp contrast to the shiny mahogany reception desk in front of which a large, wall-sized mirror hung. She wasn't sure if she was in a hotel lobby or an old western saloon. The room smelled musty and old. To Special Ed, there was a confounding aroma of truth and lies.

Gilded framed paintings lined the walls: Mona Lisa posing with a dinner fork-holding farmer from the American Gothic; Whistler's Mother rocking her chair in the Sistine Chapel; Washington crossing the Delaware on a Starry Night; Botticelli's Venus coming to life at the Last Supper.

"May I help you?"

Standing behind the reception desk stood Bertha Blooze, a rather stout woman, her hair pulled back under a red and white polka-dot bandana, her pug nose appearing to have been broken more than once. She plopped two shot glasses decisively on the desk in front of her (or was it a bar?), pulled the plug from a whiskey bottle with her teeth, and poured two drinks. She drank them both.

"What can I do for you?"

"My friend Special Ed and I are awfully tired," said Lakshmi. "We've been traveling for a long 'time' on Ye Olde Unintended Consequences Trail. And one of the unintended consequences is we came upon your establishment. I guess we could use a room."

"A room, you say," the proprietor said. Her pugilistic arms worked in quick circles as she wiped the counter with a rag. "What does a room represent to you?"

"Represent? I'm afraid I don't understand."

"A room can mean many things. It can connote the security of a mother's womb; it may imply a prison. For some, it would symbolize one's inner psyche while, to an artist, it might reflect one's sense of spatial design. Which is it for you?"

"I guess," said Lakshmi, "it represents a place where I can get a bath and a good night's sleep."

"To sleep, perchance to dream," spoke the American Gothic farmer on the wall.

"In the context of the soliloquy you quote, 'sleep' symbolizes death," Mona Lisa chimed in. "The orator you reference expresses his ambiguity toward death, while dreams represent his fear of the unknown. He yearns for a dreamless sleep but fears that in death, his earthly torments will continue in his dreams."

"And which is it for you, my dear?" asked Whistler's Mother, rocking her chair in the Sistine Chapel. "To be or not to be; that *is* the question."

"I choose to be." Lakshmi wrinkled her brow at this line of inquiry.

"However," declared Venus, sitting at the Last Supper, "you, Lakshmi Jackson, are in the midst of a dream. Therefore, are you truly *being* right now or are you simply a product of your own imagination? Here, have a wafer and a glass of wine. They're the body and blood of our Savior."

"Really? How did you manage to keep them fresh all these years? And sorry. To each his own, but I'm totally not into cannibalism."

The painted characters on the walls shouted in unison: "It's a METAPHOR!!!"

Special Ed gobbled up the wafer Venus gave him and he gobbled up Lakshmi's too. Sometimes, he didn't understand people. It was obvious to him that the wafers were not anyone's body. They were just wafers and they tasted pretty good. Not as good as the jerky Lakshmi sometimes gave him, but still… He wondered if the wafers *could* have come from somebody's ground-up fingernails or maybe from something inside someone's nose. But he had his doubts.

As for the wine they called blood, he'd drunk blood before and this most assuredly was not blood—unless it came from some weird space alien that Lakshmi made up with her thought molecules. No, it couldn't be blood. It tasted sweet and bitter at the same "time," and blood tasted much more delicious than this.

When Bertha Blooze saw Special Ed didn't like the wine, she gave him a bowl of water, but then the people on the wall started a rambling conversation about the water representing their Savior on the cross, and him rising from the dead, and transformation, and so forth. Special Ed thought it best not to bother his brain with these things, so he focused his mind on the acrid aroma of truth and lies in the room, which nobody else seemed to notice.

Lakshmi pondered Venus' previous query about dreams versus "reality," and she continued. "To answer your question, Ms. Venus, I don't know if I'm a product of my own imagination, but I'm a product of my thought molecules."

"Thought molecules…" Bertha Blooze plucked a hair from her chin and considered. "Don't you realize that 'thought molecules' are merely a literary device to describe the author's conception of how our conscious and unconscious thoughts intertwine, creating a vast array of perceptions we define as 'reality'? In introducing the motif of 'thought molecules,' the author did not claim to have looked under a microscope and have actually *seen* little amoeba-like creatures swimming around. He could have chosen an alternative symbol such as 'thought salad' or 'thought soup.' But 'salad' implies larger, more solid objects than the author intended to suggest. And 'soup' is such a tired cliche. No, the author is quite pleased with his choice of 'thought molecules' as a means of evoking the image of fluidity he wishes to convey. But please! Don't take this literally. Why, everybody?"

"It's a METAPHOR!!!"

*

"Here's a list of our rooms." Bertha pushed what appeared to be a dinner menu in front of Lakshmi. "We have several themes available."

Lakshmi perused the list. The first room to catch her eye was the *Moby Dick* room. The text read:

Join Captain Ahab in his quest to vanquish the Great White Whale, symbolizing man's hunger for God-like powers; his ambition to dominate nature; his ambivalent relationship to spirituality; and his ambiguity toward sex. Sleep in the Moby Dick *room and discover for yourself.*

Another tempting choice was the *Mississippi River* room which was thus described:

Aah, the great River of Life and all that. Immerse yourself in one of the all-'time' epic metaphors for life, nature, fertility, and the passage of "time."

The next listing said:

If the Mississippi River *isn't your metaphor of choice, try traveling down the* Highway of Life. *Take a trip On the Road, where Life is a Highway, where you might meet The Gambler who'll tell you "when to hold 'em and when to fold 'em." Head down Highway 61 where Mack the Finger tells Louie the King, "I've got forty red, white, and blue shoestrings." What better metaphor for the mystery of life than a lyric that leaves you scratching your head?*

But when all was said and done, Lakshmi and Special Ed chose the *Garden of Eden* room. Truth be told, Lakshmi was a bit weary of nothing-is-what-it-seems, and she just wanted some peace and quiet in what appeared to be a beautiful, green, abundant garden. Special Ed was in total accord with her sentiment.

"All this sideways thinking is making my brain hurt," he said.

*

George Washington had lost the *Garden of Eden* room key. "I cannot tell a lie," he said. "I was charged with being the keeper of the key, but when I went to throw a stone across the Delaware, I mistook the key for a stone and I threw it. It must have been the darkness of the Starry Night."

The metaphor was not lost on Bertha Blooze. "Of course, Washington being the 'Father of Our Country' represents a paternal figure at minimum. More likely, he's a surrogate for God. This incident speaks to our misconception that we can rely on God to possess the 'key' to our problems. The key to the *Garden of Eden* room is the key to knowledge, the key to beauty, and incidentally, the key to sin, debauchery, and a fall from grace. Which begs the question: Why in the name of Beetlejuice did you throw the key away, George?"

"I'm sorry, Bertha. My bad. But no crying over spilled milk, as the metaphor says. We'll just have to knock."

"Knock?!" she exclaimed. "What good will that do?"

"Haven't you read the Text?" Washington recited:

"Ask, and it will be given to you; seek, and you will find; knock, and it will be opened to you. For everyone who asks receives, and the one who seeks finds, and to the one who knocks it will be opened."

"Well," said Bertha, "let's test your premise and see how it holds up. Lakshmi, Special Ed, this way."

George Washington interjected. "Before you go, Lakshmi, would you like to come with me and skip that perfect skipping rock of yours across the Delaware?"

"Aah, the perfect skipping rock," said Bertha. "Now *there's* a metaphor!"

"Our quixotic quest for perfection," said the farmer, "with the tragic knowledge that it can never be achieved."

"But still a symbol of hope," added Mona Lisa.

"And," continued Whistler's Mother, rocking in the Sistine Chapel, "with Lakshmi's reluctance to skip her perfect skipping rock, we recognize that the journey is more important than the end result."

"And I thought it was just a skipping rock," Lakshmi said as she fingered the rock in her pocket. "Thank you, Mr. Washington, but I'd like to hold onto my perfect skipping rock a little bit longer."

"I rest my case," said Whistler's Mother.

"Well, come along then." Bertha Blooze fidgeted with an empty key chain. "Let's go knock on the door of the *Garden of Eden* room.

*

Knock, knock.

"Don't come in yet," called two startled voices from the other side.

Bertha ignored the request. She tried the door, it readily opened, and she walked right in. As Lakshmi and Special Ed stood at the threshold, they were greeted by the sight of a naked man and a naked woman scurrying around the room, trying to find a fig leaf.

As the reader might predict, the *Garden of Eden* room was lush with fruit trees, green foliage, and the fragrant perfume of a thousand colorful flowers. There also happened to be Adam and Eve standing in front of the bed with fig leaves now securely in place. Eve was holding a partially eaten apple. Coiled at their feet was a snake. Adam spake:

"The author depicted me as having been created by God in His image. In his rather minimalist style, the author did not describe the tools with which God built me, nor did he (I assume the author was a *he*) explain how God managed to extract my rib without anesthesia in order to build my female partner. But as the story you are currently inhabiting has made you well aware, such details can be superfluous when dealing in metaphor."

Eve chimed in: "Once the author rather clumsily contrived to have God build me out of a human rib (and yes, Adam, the author *was* a man!), he wrote about a very nice garden where God said we could live."

"Here's where da story sort o' falls apart," said the snake. "I think the author got stuck, or maybe he's under a deadline. Who knows? But he makes up this part about a 'Tree of Knowledge,' and how they wasn't supposed to eat from da tree. But then I comes along and tempts the lady, as if she don't have a mind of her own. Anyways, she eats, he eats, and then they gets to know each other."

"In a biblical sense," said Adam.

"The story goes on," said Eve. "It's rife with symbolism. The author has God kick us out of the garden and make my boyfriend here get a job. He makes childbirth so painful, it's a miracle any woman would want a baby. Just goes to show the power of hormones—although the book doesn't talk about that."

Adam continued. "Also, the author doesn't address the issue of having babies by incest. If he'd thought it through, he would have known that nothing good would come of me impregnating a woman who came from my own rib. No wonder my son Cain killed his brother Abel. Their genetic chain was all screwed up to begin with. And then the author acts surprised."

Eve's turn: "So then, Cain ups and marries his sister! What could go wrong there? It's a good thing this book we're in is a metaphor. If we were to take it literally, I'd say it's totally predictable that the human race has gone insane, what with all those incestuous roots."

"Don't forget me," said the snake. "The author makes up this part about God punishing me by makin' me crawl around on the ground. That's so unimaginative. If I was writin' the story, I coulda come up with something a lot more clever. I woulda had me standin' on my head. Now, *that* woulda been brilliant!"

"God also said we would die the day we ate the apple," added Adam. "But the author made me live for 930 years! Just goes to show he didn't have any better sense of 'time' than you do."

While Adam, Eve, and the serpent recounted their tale, Lakshmi and Special Ed had cautiously entered the room. "I have to admit," she said shyly, "there are so many holes in your story, I don't know where to start. It seems rather... unbelievable."

"That's because," Adam, Eve, the snake, and Bertha said in unison, "it's a METAPHOR!!!"

Taking another bite of her apple, Eve elaborated. "Here in Metaphor Hotel, it's incumbent upon us to distinguish figurative from literal."

"You see," continued Adam, "all of us here are products of a metaphorical tale. I would posit that someone who inhabits a story in which there's a Hospital for the Ironically Challenged, a Doldrum Bridge, and a Metaphor Hotel, is not well-positioned to question the credibility of our narrative."

"He who lives in a glass house shouldn't throw stones," observed the snake.

Eve: "That's a metaphor wrapped in a cliche."

"I suppose you have a point," Lakshmi conceded. "But still, I can't help but wonder, Adam, if God made you go to work after He kicked you out of the garden, what did you do for a living for over 900 years? Did you ever retire? Were you able to collect unemployment?"

Meanwhile, Special Ed and the snake had invented a fine game. Special Ed would dance, crouch, and bounce around the coiled serpent, while the serpent would lash out with his forked tongue within an inch of the leaping and dodging

Special Ed. The frolic came to a premature end when Special Ed sprang backwards and crashed into an apple tree, causing the forbidden fruit to become dislodged and rain down upon the inhabitants' heads.

"Okay, looks like it's 'time' to go," announced Bertha. "Adam...Eve...let's get out of our customers' hair. They need some sleep."

As they began to make their exit, however, a compelling question took root in Lakshmi's mind—a theological riddle, if you will—a conundrum so profound that she knew she would enjoy no peace until she had a definitive answer. So, as Adam and Eve were departing the *Garden of Eden*, she posed this final query:

"How do you get those fig leaves to stay on?"

*

One night of rest at Metaphor Hotel proved insufficient for Lakshmi and Special Ed to recharge their batteries (metaphorically speaking), but it renewed their determination to proceed on their journey. It had been a tumultuous night. Lakshmi's stomach hurt from the numerous fallen apples she'd eaten. There had been a loud thunderstorm. Some madman kept shouting from the ceiling in a deep baritone, threatening to "smite" her.

"Time" to depart Metaphor Hotel.

Back in the lobby, she bid farewell to Bertha Blooze and her companions in the paintings. Special Ed looked around for his serpent buddy, but he was nowhere to be found. Adam and Eve had vanished too. Lakshmi and Special Ed searched the hallways, hoping to find their friends for a final goodbye. The mystery was solved when they came upon the *Garden of Eden* room. The door was closed and the sign hanging from the knob said: Do Not Disturb.

With Hotel Metaphor in their rearview mirror (metaphorically speaking), Lakshmi and Special Ed set out to continue their journey, wondering what new adventures beckoned..

"Q Demon's fingers flew over the neck spinning his licks
snatched straight from hell."

15. MARK QUESTION AND THE QUESTION MARKS

A disclaimer by the author; Lakshmi and Special Ed encounter an unusual rock band; Mark Question introduces the band members who, along with their leader, discuss some disturbing theories; Lakshmi is taken in.

AT THIS JUNCTURE, we may be well-advised to take a quick respite from our saga and examine the plausibility of the events we have recounted thus far. The author is sensitive to criticism the reader might raise regarding the veracity of certain aspects of our tale. The previous discussion of metaphors notwithstanding, it is conceivable that certain audience members, due to an inadequate historical grounding or deficiency of imagination, might find literary devices such as a Doldrum Bridge, a Trail of Unintended Consequences, or a Metaphor Hotel, to be a bit of a stretch.

However, as shall be demonstrated in the proceeding chapter, no elements of this story exceed natural boundaries as drastically as those we witness in every day "real" life. Therefore, when characters, situations, and opinions strain the storyteller's credibility to the breaking point, it will be incumbent upon this author to inoculate himself by adopting the following procedure:

Whenever a character, situation, or opinion is presented that is based on true events, actual quotes, documented facts, or real people, an asterisk (*) will be strategically applied to indicate that, no, the author is not simply pulling an arbitrary musing from a random orifice; rather, his prose is grounded in the foundation of what we have come to perceive as "reality."

With that caveat, let us return to the breadcrumbs of Lakshmi Jackson's dream world and follow where they lead.

*

Lakshmi's thought molecules landed her with Special Ed on the crest of a high hill, from which they observed a village nestled in a valley far below. Emanating from the little hamlet was a turbulent cacophony which sounded like the hybrid mating of a 200-car collision with a nuclear holocaust. As they descended the hill, Lakshmi's thought molecules rendered her and Special Ed the sole occupants of an immense stadium. There, they discovered the source of the noise which emanated from an ear-shattering, bone-crunching, soul-crushing rock band whose members leaped and dashed across a high stage in the manner of a gerbil family in heat. They performed before a ten-foot high wall of amplifiers and an even larger screen, flashing this logo in bright orange lights:

¿Q?

We recall the Spirit Guides in Chapter 1, who lovingly lifted Lakshmi from her boat and toward the forked trail. On first glance, the band in Question may have borne a superficial resemblance to those ancient benevolent souls, what with their painted faces and otherworldly presence. However, upon closer observation, one would be forced to conclude that this crew that confronted Lakshmi was either a collection of overaged Halloween trick 'r treaters or the main attraction at a Charles Manson theme park.

The faces were painted white: white as bleach, white as death; the eyes were surrounded by surrealistic paint splashes the color of crazy; the hair flowed down their shoulders, nightmare black; the lips were crimson as fresh blood, which in the lead singer's case *was*, in fact, fresh blood which dripped from his red-stained teeth and down his chin. In his hands, he brandished a bat whose head he had gleefully bitten off.*

Special Ed yelled, "Go away! Stop making such a racket! Go away!"

But nobody could hear him above the wall of screeching guitars, pulverizing drums, and shrieking voices. And *had* they heard, the odds of the band members heeding Special Ed's admonitions would be equal to the chances of them becoming vegan nuns.

Upon spying our two seekers, the lead singer glared down from the stage with soulless eyes that reminded Lakshmi of dry ice. A tattoo—no, a brand—was burned deep into his bare chest, exhibiting the logo: ¿Q?* The music stopped. He threw away the headless bat.

"What **Q**uixotic mission brings you **Q**uirky little beings to my **Q**uaint little town of ¿**Q**? No **Q**uestion, you must be Musi**Q** lovers."

"Actually, sir, we're seeking the River of Truth. My name is Lakshmi Jackson. This is Special Ed. I'm his human."

Special Ed yelled at the man, "Go away! I don't like you! Go away!"

The only thing the singer heard was "bark bark bark," but the dog's message was clear. Conversely, Special Ed understood the man all too well, regardless of the words he heard, which were: "Blubberty blubberty blub."

The band leader wiped the bat blood from his face and reached out a smeared hand for Lakshmi to shake. "And I, of course, am the one and only Mark Question. So nice to make your acQuaintance."

"Nice to meet you, Mr. Question," said Lakshmi, wiping the blood off her hands as Special Ed continued to yell, "Go away!"

"Aah yes, the River of Truth," said he. "You've come to the right place. Truth River…" he crooned, "wider than a mile…

"I will have you sailing on the River of Truth Quite Quickly. But first, I would be remiss if I didn't acQuaint you with the members of my Quartet. Ladies and gentlemen, I give you The Question Marks:

"To my right," he pointed dramatically, "on lead guitar—he thrashes, he shreds, he stole every note he plays straight from the Devil himself—put your hands together fo-o-or…. Q Demon!" *

Q Demon leaped to the lip of the stage in an ominous crouch, guitar pointing directly from his grinding crotch toward Lakshmi, his snake-like tongue undulating to the rhythm of his blurred fingers as they flew over the neck, spinning licks snatched directly from hell.

Q Demon finished his fiendish riffs and bore his painted eyes into Lakshmi's. "You want the River of Truth?" he Queried. "How Quaint! Here's the truth for you: Remember the moon landing? It was a hoax! Doesn't it seem Queer to you that there are no stars in the picture? Have you no Qualms that there is no blast crater under the landing module? Haven't you noticed the Quirky ways the shadows fall? I Quote: 'It's well documented that NASA was often badly managed and had poor Quality control. But as of 1969, we could suddenly perform manned flight upon manned flight? With complete success?' I think not," said Q Demon with a self-satisfied flourish.*

Resuming his center stage stance, Mark **Q**uestion continued his introductions. "And to my left on bass, we have the King of Karnage, Lord of the Roar, the Sulton of Slaughter himself...let's give it up fo-o-or...**Q** Slaughter!" *

Q Slaughter strutted forward, laying down a bottom-heavy beat that caused the empty stadium to quake. He s**Q**uinted darkly as he growled in a voice as low as his bass. "That shooting at that elementary school where twenty kids and six teachers was *supposedly* killed? It was fake. No one died, ya know. It was actually staged by the guvment so they could put the s**Q**ueeze on you an' take away yer guns." *

"And now, ladies and gentlemen," **Q**uoth Mark **Q**uestion, "coming at you straight from his record-breaking Underworld Tour, the Pounder of Percussion... the Drummer of Death...the Beat Butcher himself: **Q** Hammerhell!"*

Strobe lights flashed on a crazed behemoth exploding behind a colossal constellation of drums, cymbals, and everything capable of making noise. **Q** Hammerhell bashed out a sequence of pummels on toms-to-snares-to-cymbals-to-bass and stopped! Suddenly, the arena became so deathly quiet, one could hear a dog bark. Which was precisely the task to which Special Ed applied himself, yelling at the band to "go away!"

Q Hammerhell gazed down at Lakshmi with a maniacal leer. "The guvment has weather weapons capable of creating tornados! That hurricane we had last week that killed thirty-three people? It was geo-engineered by the Air Force!" * He whacked his bass drum.

"Global warming is a hoax made up by the World Bank to control the world economy through a carbon tax!" * He bashed his snare.

"The reason there's so many gay people now is cuz it's a chemical warfare operation! The guvment is encouraging homosexuality with chemicals so people won't have kids!

They're puttin' chemicals in the water that's turnin' frogs into the gay!" * He crashed his symbol.

"There now," said Mark Question. "What d'ya think about that?"

"I think we should make a skiddadle," said Special Ed, tugging on Lakshmi's arm. "Special Ed most assuredly doesn't like these people. They smell like a burnt-down house."

But Lakshmi couldn't look away. She was drawn to the spectacle like the proverbial moth to a flame; like a witness to a train wreck. The victim of a hypnotist's spell, she stared at Mark Question with mesmerized fascination. He dangled a watch chain and swung it in pendulum oscillations before her attentive eyes.

"Did you know," Mark Question Questioned, "that there's a cabal of Satan-worshiping pedophiles running a global child sex-trafficking ring that's plotting against MISTER BIGLY?" *

"There is?" exclaimed Lakshmi.

"It's true! But listen! There's more: The anti-BIGLY politicians, movie stars, and billionaires secretly rule the world while engaging in human trafficking and harvesting a life-extending chemical from the blood of abused children!" *

*

"They do?"

"That's right! And we have to support MISTER BIGLY because he alone can stop them! He's waging a secret battle that only we, in the little town of ¿Q? know anything about. He's fighting to expose the criminal mob and their deep state collaborators in the government and in the press, and send them off to a secret prison where they'll never be heard from again!" *

"He alone can stop them," said Lakshmi.

But Mark Question wasn't finished. "I have one word for you, Lakshmi Jackson. It's a classified code word that only the initiated are allowed to hear. Are you ready to hear the word?"

"I'm ready," said Lakshmi drowsily.

"Pizza. The word is 'pizza.' Listen: We have intercepted messages from MISTER BIGLY's enemies using the word 'pizza,' which everybody knows is code for 'pedophilia.' * They planned to meet at Ping Pong Pizzeria, which is a meeting ground for Satanic ritual abuse.* They were using the pizza joint as a front for human trafficking and a child sex ring." *

"I had no idea," said Lakshmi.

"But I'm not Quite finished with my story," he continued. "Do you know who the ring leader is?"

"Who?" Her eyes were drooping.

"Why, it's none other than your dear friend, Sophia Wise."

"How terrible," she murmured vacantly.

"Lakshmi," yelled Special Ed. "Let's run away far! I can't smell the truth at all. It smells so bad here, I don't even want to roll in it!"

"Tell your dog to shut up," said Mark Question. "The only thing more annoying than a deep-state non-believer is a barking dog."

"Special Ed," she commanded. "No bark!"

"Wait a minute!" cried Special Ed. "I thought we had a deal."

"No bark!" she ordered again.

"Now," said Mark Question, "follow me into the inner sanctum of ¿Q?, where you will be initiated into the ways of our town. And when we have completed your training, we will send you forth to destroy the enemy of MISTER BIGLY, and the enemy of the Free Nation: Sophia Wise."

"Yes..." said Lakshmi dreamily. "Sophia Wise...enemy of the Free Nation..."

"Hammerhell!" Mark Question shouted. "Do something with that damn dog!"

"Mark Question was tearing his man cave to shreds."

16. TALK RADIO

A musing about the Infinite Void; Lakshmi
enters Mark Question's domain; Mark
Question hocks his products; a brief visit from
MISTER BIGLY; the practice of applying an
asterisk (*) to events, people, and statements
categorized as "stranger than fiction"
continues.

LAKSHMI'S THOUGHT MOLECULES took a much-
needed hiatus, and she descended into the Infinite Void —
presumably the same Void which sandwiches us before
we are born and after we die. There is no such thing as
matter in the Void, no such thing as *"time,"* no such thing
as *thing* when there is *nothing*; therefore we have no idea
how much "time" Lakshmi spent there — whatever *"there"*
means. Which begs the question: Where *was* Lakshmi when
she exited consciousness and entered the Void? Why, in the
Wonder Bread of a Void Sandwich, if you will.

When Lakshmi's thought molecules began to regroup, she
found Mark Question leading her into a cramped room
which appeared to be a scientific laboratory that doubled
as a recording studio. The centerpiece of the cubicle was a
48-channel analog recording and mixing console, replete
with 48 motorized faders, onboard signal processing, pure

drive preamps, and E-series EQ. Either that, or it was an airplane flight control deck. Hard to tell which.

Perched on top of what turned out to be a mixing console after all, were bubbling canisters labeled "iodine" and "magnesium oxide" and "citric acid." Scattered around the studio were a cluttered array of computers, TV screens, laser instruments, and gerbils in cages. The gerbil cages were labeled: "Q Demon," "Q Slaughter," and "Q Hammerhell."

Lakshmi didn't notice that her thought molecules had rearranged Mark Question. No longer did he affect the bearing of a slasher movie hallucination. Rather, he now presented as a bald-headed, block-headed, bull-necked, barrel-chested, obsolete ex-football player looking for some blameless bystander to bowl over.*

The black t-shirt was several sizes too small, clinging to his torso like a cowboy rider adhering to a bucking brahma bull; the pants crotch bulged like a boxer's fist, suggesting either the gifts of a man tremendously endowed or the answer to the mystery of what had become of his other sock. The trimmed salt and pepper goatee and mustache framed a jaw that ground furiously, as if the owner were chewing up the world and spitting it out. The singular aspect of Mark Question that remained from his previous presentation was the crazed glare emanating from the two windows of his tormented soul.*

Strewn about the room was a shambles of discarded pizza boxes, crushed beer cans, broken whiskey bottles, stubbed out cigarettes, and scattered amphetamines. A few hopped-up rats scurried about the wreckage, scooping up the left-overs.

"Sit down, Lakshmi," said Mark Question. "I have a show to do. Watch and learn."

He plopped into his ergonomic chair, twisted a few console knobs, pushed a few buttons, leaned into a microphone which stood before him, and with the "ON THE AIR" sign flashing red, he wasted little "time" with introductions.

"Hello, Questionable Patriots! Today, I want to talk to you about my special line of Brainiac elixir which is perfect ammunition for anyone who believes the Armageddon is near! Top scientists and researchers agree: the government is attacking us with toxic weapons in our food and water supply that are designed to make us fat, sick, and stupid!*

"But now, you can fight back! With my new line of **Q-Brainiac PLUS**, we've taken it to the next level. Where do you think I get my brilliance and stamina to relentlessly carry out my God-given mission to make the world safe from tyranny; to vanquish every foreigner who would rob you of your liberty; to destroy every terrorist who's coming to steal your guns, rape your children, and dominate the world? Where do my super powers come from? Why, I take **Q-Brainiac PLUS** elixir before every hard-hitting show!*

"Do your patriotic duty and join the millions of Questionable Patriots who are making the world safe from the deep state demagogues and order your **Q-Brainiac PLUS** today without delay!

"But wait! There's more! If you order your **Q-Brainiac PLUS** elixir today, we'll send you our special formula of **Q-HardMan Virility and Vitality Solution** for half price! **HardMan**! I use it to maximize my manliness when working 14 hours a day in my lonely crusade for liberty! Folks, let me tell you, **HardMan** works so well that I actually had to stop taking it before I went on the air or I would get more virility than you Questionables could handle!*

"Trust me, Questionable Patriots. One dose of **HardMan** and your wife will wonder what's gotten into you! Then she'll wonder what's gotten into *her*!"

BA-DUM-BUM went the pre-recorded drums.

The phone rang. Mark **Q**uestion picked it up, and a look of incredulousness passed over his face. "Yes sir," he said. "Very good, sir. Just give me a minute to dial you in.

"**Q**uestionable Patriots," he announced, "we have a call from my best friend, *your* best friend, and the World Champion of Truth, Justice, and the Free Nation way! The one and only... MISTER BIGLY!"

Mark **Q**uestion turned a couple knobs, pulled down a fader and pushed one up; and there, on the overhead screen appeared the unmistakable visage of MISTER BIGLY chewing a cheeseburger. One could see the soggy remnants on his tongue which protruded from his masticating mouth like a lizard slithering through a sloshy bog. He spoke with his mouth full:

"Mark's products are tremendush! They're almost as tremendush as *my* very tremendush products. Mark's a very tremendush guy. Everybody knows he's not as tremendush as me, but he's tremendush too. But I'm the most very tremendush, by the way."

"Thank you, sir! Did you try out that free sample of **HardMan** I sent you?"

"I started out by looking at certain things and I've been working very, very carefully, very strongly. Nobody has done anything like I've been able to do. And everything I took over was a mess. It was a broken country in so many ways. In so many ways. I've done a job, the likes of which nobody has ever done. We'll see what happens." *

"There you have it, **Q**uestionable Patriots," Mark **Q**uestion gushed. "Don't take it from *me*. Take it from MISTER BIGLY! You'll never hear a more ringing endorsement of my products than you just heard from him!"

Lakshmi sat in a far corner of the room, flanked by two of Mark **Q**uestion's **Q**uestionables. They were burly men, the sleeveless arms slathered with tattoos, the bill of their

¿Q? ball caps turned to the back of their heads. They held Lakshmi's arms gently but firmly, and it didn't seem that they planned to relinquish their grip.

As she watched the host rant and rave through his marathon radio show, her thought molecules slipped, slid, and melded. Somewhere between warnings that vaccines cause autism and pitches for his new line of bulletproof vests,* Mark Question reconfigured into a lumbering brute resembling a cartoon character who was once a favorite of her grandparents: a blunt-headed caveman by the name of Alley Oop.

*

Like buckets of various colored paints poured in a pan, Lakshmi's thought molecules swirled and transformed. She found herself floating near the ceiling of an old, dilapidated tool shed with rotting wooden boards leaning every which way. She peered down, and there on the floor lay Special Ed whimpering in a corner, looking thoroughly bereft.

Around his neck was a spiked collar to which a chain was clipped, extending four feet and hooking to a bolt in the wall. He lay with the chain stretched taut, body flat to the ground, head between his outstretched paws. The collar spikes dug into his neck, but he didn't care. He wanted to be as far from the wall as the chain would allow him to go. He stared ahead with mournful, dog-brown eyes.

The men who had taken him there were not kind. They had handled him roughly, cuffing and kicking him, and saying cruel things. Special Ed didn't hear much more than "blubberty blubberty blub," yet he understood everything he needed to know.

What the captors discussed among themselves was Mark Question's intent to launch a ground-breaking experiment targeting Special Ed's Honesty Intelligence Quotient. As has been previously noted, Special Ed possessed a highly developed aptitude for truth-telling. Mark **Q**uestion meant to extract Special Ed's brain and isolate the chemical that endowed him with this prodigious gift. If successful, he mused, he could inject the entire water supply of the Free Nation with the solution, thus rendering the populace with a distinct disadvantage in their attempts to discern truth from fiction. Or, metaphorically speaking, it could cause them to run blindly into the field every "time" Mark **Q**uestion faked throwing the ball.

*

While Special Ed quietly whined in the corner and awaited his fate, Lakshmi's thought molecules returned her to the recording studio where all manner of chaos had ensued. For, Mark **Q**uestion, in his latest incarnation as a hairy hulking troglodyte, was tearing his man cave to shreds.

Sophia showered the assailants with the "time"-less beauty of Johann Sebastian Bach.

17. SOPHIA ARRIVES

Mark Question throws a tantrum; the Question Marks prepare to perform surgery; Sophia Wise communes with Bach; Special Ed gets a reprieve; the author's employment of asterisks continues.

"**B**RING ME Sophia Wise!"

The mangy Homo Erectus was on a rampage. The cudgel he wielded in his meaty paws was a woolly mammoth femur capable of inflicting lethal damage, and Mark Question was in the process of making full use of its potential.

Lakshmi cowered in a corner as the rank-smelling caveman, clad in saber-tooth tiger skin, his hair a mad tangle of oily mats, his deep-set eyes searching maniacally around the room for something to destroy, launched a systematic riot of clobbering everything in sight. He hoisted the club two-handed above his head, his hairy, outstretched arms the width of a linebacker's thighs.

"Sophia Wise is the Satanic ringleader of the pedophilic Ping Pong Pizzeria!" *

BAM! The cudgel came down on the console. Large fragments flew across the room, bounced off the ceiling, and landed in Lakshmi's trembling lap.

"Sophia Wise has engineered the murder of thousands of innocent people, including Ambassador Ben Gazzy!" *

BLAM! He took a mighty, Ruthian swing at the mike and hit it out of the park.

"EMAILS! EMAILS! EMAILS! Sophia Wise wrote over 3,000 EMAILS!" * he bellowed.

BOOM! Leaping with shaggy bare feet on the fractured console, Mark Question bashed the overhead TV screen which exploded like the 4th of July around the studio. He lumbered across the room, stopping to hyperventilate his malodorous caveman breath just inches from Lakshmi's face.

"BRING ME SOPHIA WISE!"

*

While Lakshmi cringed in the corner of Mark Question's recording studio, Special Ed lay chained on the floor of the tool shed, trying to reconnect with his friend. No matter how far he scattered his thought molecules, he could not find hers. There were moments when he thought he felt their molecules mixing, but each "time," she faded into a depressing gray, and what remained was an image of a psychotic Neanderthal.

The shed door creaked open. In walked Q Demon, Q Slaughter, and Q Hammerhell, no longer in the personas of deranged rock musicians, but rather, dressed in full hazmat suits and bearing an array of surgical instruments.

"Let's get 'r done," said Q Demon. "Mark Question is in a hurry."

"Has anybody ever extracted a brain before?" asked Q Slaughter.

"What's the big deal?" said Q Hammerhell. "Just cut his head open and take the sucker out. Do it without anesthesia.

We'll do a groundbreaking scientific study to see how he reacts."

*

Sophia Wise lounged on a love seat, serenely strumming her mandolin. It was as plain as the tattoos on her body and face that she was weary after another day in the town of Red Rock, supervising the distribution of food to the needy, attending to medical requirements at the clinic, and welcoming new refugees fresh from their escape from Chosen Leader Delbert Thorne's nuclear disaster.

Without missing a beat in the music, she brushed her long purple hair away from her mandolin. She had only recently taken to dying her hair again after a protracted hiatus. It only required half as much dye now, for she had recently shaved the right side of her head. However, she was still swearing off new tattoos, and truth be told, she had pretty much run out of room.

The music with which she communed was courtesy of the master: Johann Sebastian Bach. For Sophia, Bach's miraculous logic and order made sense of her absurd and chaotic world. His perfect balance of mind and spirit planted her feet firmly on the ground while causing her heart to soar. The elegant beauty of Bach's inventions made her eyes well with tears as if she were watching the sun rise or the birth of a child. Sophia played Bach like a celebration; like a meditation; like a prayer.

On this evening, Sophia was playing Bach's Chaconne. Like certain Indian ragas, Sophia believed the Chaconne should only be played at night. She might have been only vaguely aware that she loved the piece because it was so much like her: Based on one simple four-measure theme, it methodically dug deeper and deeper with each of its 64 variations, tenaciously laying bare every anguish and exultation of the human soul. Gone were the clever key modulations; the introduction of new motifs; the fugal complexity. Gone was any attempt to hold the listener with pretense, trick, or gimmick. What remained was a plodding, relentless quest for Truth. The Chaconne left no scraps on the table; when one finished playing it, there was nothing left to say.

Lakshmi's thought molecules caused Sophia to materialize just as she was segueing from the fierce D minor Chaconne variations into the celestial elegance of the D major midsection. The music floated tranquilly in the air along with Sophia, who drifted through "time" and space until she arrived, hovering beneath the ceiling of the shed where Special Ed's lobotomy was imminent. A trace of an angelic smile lit her face as the music from her mandolin sprinkled down on the participants like fairy dust.

Q Demon and Q Slaughter rolled on the ground in a violent scrum with a muzzled and thrashing Special Ed. Q Demon clung desperately to his wrestler's headlock hold while Q Slaughter did his best to maintain a grip on Special Ed's gyrating hindquarters. Special Ed was not going down without a fight.

"Hold him down!" commanded Q Hammerhell, wielding a scalpel. "Keep him still!" He bent over the outmatched dog and lowered the blade over his head. He was but an inch away when he heard the music.

"What's that?" he whispered, looking toward the source.

Q Demon and Q Slaughter heard it too, and gazing heavenward, they softened their grip. Sophia hovered over them, showering the assailants with beauty, love, the divine wisdom and "time"-less truth of Johann Sebastian Bach.

They relented. As one, the three men stood, mouths hanging open and eyes flooding tears. They gaped mesmerized as Sophia continued to spin her tune, a beatific glow adorning her face.

As the maestro's 15-minute melodrama wound down to its inevitable conclusion, not with fireworks but more like a master carpenter hammering in the final nail (or like God on the seventh day, declaring the world "very good"), Sophia wafted ghostly to the ground. With eyes locked into the stares of her incredulous audience, she dramatically rendered the final notes. The room lay eerily still, sonic jewels still echoing off the walls. Sophia broke the silence.

"Now *that*," she declared, "is *Truth!*"

The gawking men nodded their assent. Tears and drool washed their faces clean. They had experienced Truth on a profound level; a Truth that knows no lies; a Truth that few humans are privy to; a Truth that usually only dogs can attain.

Sophia picked a ball off the ground and faked a throw out the shed door. The three men went running after it. Then she bent down to a wiggle-waggling Special Ed, removed his muzzle, and released him from his chain.

"C'mon, Special Ed," she said. "Let's go find Lakshmi."

"Throw me the ball, Sophia! Throw me the ball!"

"At the front of the upside-down jostling mob strode Mark Question."

18. STORMING THE PALACE

Alone in the ravaged recording studio,
Lakshmi decodes some hidden messages;
a large mob of Questionables breaks in;
Mark Question leads the Minions to BIGLY
Palace; although the author's practice of
employing asterisks to indicate factual basis
will no longer be applied, the principal of art
imitating life continues.

IT MAY TAKE A WHILE for Sophia and Special Ed to materialize in Lakshmi's thought molecules again. So, as they slowly drift in the unconscious void, let's race ahead of them toward their inevitable destination in Lakshmi's dream. We shall trust they'll catch up in due "time."

Following the disorienting transformations of Mark Question from Death Metal band leader to crazed radio jockey to raging Homo Erectus, and on the heels of Caveman Question's cacophonous trashing of his studio, Lakshmi's rattled psyche possessed an understandable urgency for introspective respite. Therefore, it may not surprise the reader that Lakshmi's thought molecules took a markedly inward turn.

Mark Question's rants had provoked many Questions in her vulnerable mind. Questions such as:

"There are 11 letters in MISTER BIGLY's name, however, **Q** is the 17th letter of the alphabet. Why the discrepancy? But…if we add in MISTER BIGLY'S *middle* name, which is ARRYAN, that adds up to 17! Wow! That's incredible!"

Kneeling on the floor of the pillaged recording studio and maneuvering into a headstand, she mulled over these thoughts:

"When MISTER BIGLY said, 'We will get through this together,' what was His secret message? Was 'together' a code for: 'To get her'? As in: To get Sophia Wise? That's the only thing that makes sense. It's so sad that more people don't understand the importance of critical thinking!"

Bouncing on her head, she paced and pondered:

"MISTER BIGLY was absolutely correct to cancel the election. The only way He could have lost would have been if the Others were allowed to vote, and everyone knows *that* wasn't going to happen. So, what would be the point?"

Standing on her head caused abundant **Q**uantities of blood to rush to her brain, providing much clarity to her thinking:

"Besides, if He were to submit Himself to an election, it could be interpreted as a sign of weakness. And if MISTER BIGLY is to achieve His goal of world domination, He must never allow himself to be seen as limp, puny, or impotent."

Lakshmi found the ball cap that Mark **Q**uestion had given her. She donned it to protect her head from the shattered glass on the floor. The cap said: I'M A BRAINWASHED BIGLY BOOSTER. She remembered Mark **Q**uestion's last words before he stormed out of his man cave:

"The only person standing in the way of MISTER BIGLY attaining His rightful rank as Undisputed Lord of the World is Sophia Wise. She must be stopped!"

*

Lakshmi heard a riotous commotion at the door. The jumbled voices of ten thousand angry men seethed like a rolling thunder cloud. Individual voices could barely penetrate the incoming roar. The walls of the studio shook and the door buckled from the human tsunami pounding on the other side.

Then, with a mighty crash, the door broke down and in poured the mob, bouncing on their heads, wielding torches, clubs, tire irons, pitchforks, and semi-automatic weapons; waving enormous flags with depictions of MISTER BIGLY sitting on his Tremendous Golden Throne; banners that read "¿Q?" and "Call me Questionable," and "I AM A BIGLY MINION," and others that simply said "I'M A BM."

These rough and rowdy men—and the author intentionally says "men" because, while there was a smattering of women who were every bit as rugged and wild as their male counterparts, let's confront the facts: this was a decidedly testosterone-soaked affair in the "time"-honored tradition of the Old Testament and the Taliban—these upside-down, ranting, chanting, cursing men wearing a most unusual variety of fashion designs proclaiming their uncompromising demand for "Freedom," their hatred for the Others, their litany of grievances against the evil socialist Sophia Wise, their allegiance to MISTER BIGLY, and their tribal conformity to individualism.

And what a display it was: Bodies splotched with tattoos that broadcast the same complaints and sentiments as the banners they waved; a swirl of hoodies, army fatigues, and bare chests splattered with blood, sweat, and spit; Halloween-like costumes representing Count Dracula, the Grim Reaper, and Freddy Krueger; shaved heads sporting waist-length beards. Think: Blackbeard the Pirate meets Yosemite Sam.

At the front of the upside-down jostling mob packed tighter than hogs in a hog farm strode Mark Question. (We use the word "strode" advisedly in that he did so as much as it's possible to "stride" on one's head while wearing elk horns.) No longer affecting the retro/paleontological/Homo Erectus image, he now sported an ensemble befitting the current state of affairs: The above-mentioned elk horns; the required Rasputin beard; the ammo belt draped over his bare chest which prominently displayed his new **BM** tattoo; the camouflage pants, the hobnail boots, and of course, the AR-15 which he waved to propel the crowd forward.

"Hurry, Lakshmi," he shouted above the roar. "MISTER BIGLY is holding a rally! No 'time' to waste!"

"Mark!" she exclaimed. "I think I've cracked the code! If you unscramble the 17 letters that spell MISTER ARRYAN BIGLY, you get SLY GRIMEY RAT BRAIN. Now it finally makes sense!"

"Let's go, Lakshmi. We don't have a moment to lose!"

Lakshmi bounced over to Mark **Q**uestion's side as he turned to exhort the crowd. "It's off to BIGLY Palace, fellow BMs!" he bellowed. "MISTER BIGLY is about to deliver an important message we must hear. He says he's going to shepherd us out of the wilderness and lead us to the Promised Land where we'll finally be free! Free from government tyranny! Free from the Others! Free from Sophia Wise! Let's go, **Q**uestionables! On to the Palace!"

And with that, Mark **Q**uestion, Lakshmi Jackson, and the rowdy thousands of **Q**uestionable BMs turned tail and stormed down BIGLY Boulevard, heading for destiny; heading for their brush with greatness; heading for BIGLY Palace where their Magnificent Leader would resolve their earthly problems, once and for all.

*

By the "time" they stormed the Palace, they were a half a million strong. Which begs the Zen **Q**uestion: What is Woodstock, minus the rock 'n' roll, minus the acid, minus the sex, minus the peace, minus the love? Why, the answer, of course, is a rally at BIGLY Palace where, the crowd was "much bigger, much much bigger than Woodstock," MISTER BIGLY would say in his later years. "That I can tell you," MISTER BIGLY would inform anyone in his jail cell who would listen. "Much much bigger. Believe me."

MISTER BIGLY

19. MISTER BIGLY'S MANIFESTO

BIGLY's Minions descend on BIGLY Palace; MISTER BIGLY addresses his flock; Sophia and Special Ed find Lakshmi and initiate an inoculation program; although no asterisks will be employed to indicate resemblance to factual events, the reader may infer that MISTER BIGLY's speech warrants one long asterisk.

THE SOLID GOLD walls of BIGLY Palace sparkled in the afternoon sun. With its ruby-studded domes reaching toward the heavens; its six marble lions standing guard; its turquoise chlorinated moat stretching for blocks; its fountain gushing in a skyward salute to the naked bronze Venus at the entrance; its splendorous, sky-scraping tower housing a magnificent 3-star hotel;* its revolving floodlights stabbing the compound with red, yellow, blue, and green illumination; with its massive neon sign above the Gothic anterior archway announcing **BIGLY PALACE**, the domain's every detail reflected MISTER BIGLY's singular conception of aesthetics, his ravenous hunger for conspicuous opulence, and his high decibel compulsion for self-promotion.

*(It could have been a 5-star hotel if the workers hadn't gone on strike. It seems MISTER BIGLY had neglected to pay

them for the previous year, and when the pipes broke there was no one willing to do the maintenance. Guests began to complain about leakage from the ceiling, mold on the walls, puddles in the carpets, and exploding toilets. To be fair, MISTER BIGLY did dispatch his two sons to repair the plumbing. But it soon became evident that expecting Rufus and Doofus to fix the plumbing was equivalent to hiring a pair of chimpanzees to fly an airplane.)

The rising tide of BIGLY's Minions crashed upon the Palace shore, an angry lynch mob in search of someone to lynch. But the passion that had propelled them to the cusp of the Palace had fulfilled its purpose. Now they needed someone to channel their raw energy and mobilize it into action; someone to tell them where to aim their fury, what to think, whom to hate. The flock needed a shepherd. Their eyes gazed twelve stories up to MISTER BIGLY's balcony.

They didn't have to wait long. The floodlights turned and unleashed their colors in great swirling bursts upon the balcony, causing the crowd to cheer in uproarious anticipation.

Magnificent fireworks exploded in the heavens. Thunderous music boomed from the hotel tower. Recognizing MISTER BIGLY's theme song, *These Boots Are Made for Walking*, the horde erupted in a sing-along frenzy, knowing their Glorious Leader was poised to emerge.

There was a brief moment of disappointment when, rather than MISTER BIGLY materializing, an elderly man in his bathrobe and slippers padded out onto the balcony looking dazed and irate.

"This is disgusting!" he spat into the microphone. "I paid good money for this hotel and I can't get any sleep! Would you guys pipe down?!"

There was as much chance of BIGLY's Minions piping down as there would be of a trout singing *These Boots Are Made for Walking*. At the moment the singer sang, "One of these days these boots are going to walk all over you," as if on cue, four of MISTER BIGLY's bodyguards materialized from the wings, converged on the hapless codger, and silently without fanfare, picked him up and dispatched him over the 12-story balcony, into the waiting crowd below. Lakshmi's thought molecules briefly turned the old man into a large rabbit and the mob became piranhas in a tank. There was a cloud of blood in the water and he was gone.

The enforcers disappeared as discretely as they had appeared. The music continued to blare. When the singer called, "Are you ready, boots? Start walkin'," His Magnificence emerged. Unlike his Minions, he stood on his own two feet, his chest puffed out.

*

He held his hands aloft, wallowing in the adulation. He smiled like a baby being burped. The caterpillar mustache above his lip squirmed in discomfort, unaccustomed to this novel variation of expression. As MISTER BIGLY gazed down upon his BMs, Lakshmi's thought molecules briefly morphed him into a fat feral cat, smugly satisfied after catching a bird.

The balcony sagged under his prodigious weight. The extra handful of MISTER BIGLY's *Tremendous Pomade* that he had applied to his impossible pompadour glistened in the scorching afternoon sun. The fresh coat of MISTER BIGLY's *Tremendous Shoe Polish and Hair Dye (Black)* was already beginning to run down his orange cheeks, causing much consternation to the caterpillar who squirmed and recoiled. Oblivious to imperfections in his visage, MISTER BIGLY waved to his herd, soaking in their adoration, pointing at selected individuals like an entertainer in a Vegas lounge act. The crowd was delirious. MISTER BIGLY basked.

He launched his opening salvo. "Do you love me?"

"WE LOVE YOU, MISTER BIGLY!" came the cry.

"Yes, but do you LOVE me?"

"WE LOVE YOU, MISTER BIGLY!"

"If you really love me, let me see you do the BIGLY Bounce."

In unison, BIGLY's Minions began bouncing on their heads. Lakshmi's thought molecules momentarily turned them into thousands of upside-down toddlers jumping on trampolines.

He turned to his four upright bodyguards with a simulated smile. "I think they *do* love me."

Behind their dark glasses they nodded, frowning straight ahead.

"I *said*, I think they *love* me. What do *you* think?"

The bodyguards replied in sing-song unison: "Everybody loves you, sir. You are the greatest leader in the history of great leaders. We are honored to be in your presence."

Back to the Minions: "Many people love me. Believe me. They say, 'Sir, what's your secret?' I say, 'I'm a *winner*. I *win*. I'm a *winner*.' I'm going to *win* that law suit. That disgusting cow who's suing me for using her song at my rallies. That 'boots' song. We'll see what happens. She's such a loser. Many people say she's a loser. I don't like losers. I like *winners*. That's why I'll *win*. I'm a *winner*, by the way. Everybody knows I'm a *winner*. I'm very rich. I've got so many billions, I need a billion accountants to count how many billions I've got. Believe me. Billions of billions. They're suing me. They say, 'Sir, you didn't pay me.' Why should I pay them when I had to pay $750 in taxes? We'll see what happens. I'm very very rich. Very very very rich. I'm tremendously rich. Richer than you'll ever be. Believe me."

MB's BMs were ecstatic. MISTER BIGLY was in top form. To show their appreciation, they did the BIGLY Bounce.

"I can make you rich too. Not as rich as me. Many people are saying that nobody will ever be as rich as me. Many people.

Believe me. The radical lib-tards wish we would go away.
They want to destroy us because we're *winners*. We *win* so
much it gets boring. Are you bored yet?"

Some BM's shouted "YES!" and some shouted "NO!" They
weren't certain if they were supposed to be bored because
they were winning so much or if they *weren't* supposed to
be bored because they were in MISTER BIGLY's presence.
It was all a bit confusing, but geniuses can be difficult to
understand. They tried to follow and prayed they wouldn't
get it wrong.

While Lakshmi and Mark Question stood on their heads at
the front of the herd, Sophia and Special Ed sifted incognito
through the crush of upside-down bodies. Walking on their
heads to blend in, they wore identical tan trench coats,
fedoras, and black sunglasses. Special Ed carried a large
briefcase, the contents of which will soon be revealed. It was
slow going, as the worshippers were packed tightly and not
inclined to give an inch. But Sophia and Special Ed were
determined to find Lakshmi.

Well into his second hour, MISTER BIGLY was just warming
up. He held above his head a thin sheet of paper. "I have in
my hand MISTER BIGLY's Bill of Goods. Many people ask
me, 'Sir, you're such a *winner*. How can I *win* like you do?'
I say, 'Buy MISTER BIGLY's Bill of Goods and find out. It
will make you a *winner* too. Not like me. Nobody *wins* like
me, by the way.' You can *win* too. To *win*, we have to get
rid of the Others. They're losers. They want to take back
everything you rightfully stole from them. It's *your* land! It's
your money! It's *your* right to stop them from voting against
me! The Others want to take away your freedom! They want
to rob you of your God-given freedom to take away their
freedom!"

Sophia and Special Ed jostled closer to the front. As the
BMs did the BIGLY Bounce, Sophia and Special Ed bounced
extra high so they could see over the crowd. Now they had
Lakshmi in their sights and their worst fears were realized.

There she was, bouncing upside-down with Mark **Q**uestion and the rest of the flock, madly cheering every non sequitur that escaped MISTER BIGLY's mouth.

"You have to cut the tiger off at the head! Catch the chicken by the tail! One way to skin a cat! And that way is to cut off its head!"

Even MISTER BIGLY's most devoted Minions scratched their puzzled heads each "time" they bounced off the ground. But, of course, they thought, "Brilliant wizardry is hard to follow." They would simply have to devote their full concentration to comprehend what their Great Leader was saying.

"What a crowd! What a crowd! You're a tremendous crowd! Much more tremendous than any crowd Sophia Wise ever got."

At the sound of her name, the BMs began to boo. This they could understand.

"Sophia Wise. You gotta cut off the head. Cut off the head. Sophia Wise." His voice was a stage whisper. "Sophia Wise. Three thousand emails. Best friends with Ben Gazzy. The Pizza Pedophile. That's what I call her. Pizza Pedophile Sophia Wise."

"BOO-OO-OO!" Righteous anger stirred the Minions. Violence was in the air. "Cut off her head! Cut off the head of Pizza Pedophile Sophia Wise!"

MISTER BIGLY's voice rose over the fevered crowd. "Pizza Pedophile Sophia Wise and her Red Rock traitors are trying to take away your freedom!"

"BOO-OO-OO!"

"They're stealing your freedom to steal their freedom!"

"BOO-OO-OO!"

"Pizza Pedophile Sophia Wise has turned Red Rock into a socialist sanctuary for the Others! They get health care! Child care! Education! They get their energy from solar and wind! They're banning privately owned nuclear weapons!"

"BOO-OO-OO!"

"Red Rock is a radical lib-tard cradle-to-grave socialist paradise! That I can tell you! Are you going to allow this to happen?"

"NO, MISTER BIGLY!"

"Are you going to stop Pizza Pedophile Sophia Wise?"

"YES, MISTER BIGLY!"

"Are you going to cut off her head?"

The lynch mob finally knew whom to lynch.

*

Sophia and Special Ed sidled up to Lakshmi, and Sophia tugged on her arm.

"Sophia!" cried Lakshmi. "What are you doing here? Look, everybody! It's the Pizza Pedo..."

Sophia quickly put her hand over Lakshmi's mouth and hoped no one heard her above the roaring crowd. Special Ed opened the briefcase he was carrying and fished out a hypodermic needle. Sophia seized the needle and jammed it into Lakshmi's arm.

"What the..."

Sophia looked Lakshmi in the eye and held her index finger to her lips, signaling silence. She whispered in Lakshmi's ear. "You and everybody here are suffering from a severe case of the BIGLY Virus. I've just inoculated you. Are you okay now?"

Lakshmi answered in a daze. "Yes, I guess I am. I don't know what came over me. I just..."

Sophia put her finger to her lips again. "You've been very very sick. Fortunately, Tyrone T. Matters, Ph.D. and his crack team of scientists at Red Rock have developed a vaccine that's 100% effective against the BIGLY Virus. Incidentally, it also cures rabies. But this gathering is a dangerous super-spreader event. We don't have a moment to lose. If we're to stop the BIGLY Virus from infecting the entire world, we have to inoculate these poor afflicted people now!"

With that, Sophia, Special Ed, and Lakshmi equally divided the vaccines contained in Special Ed's briefcase and began their inoculation program. To each person whose arm they stuck, they handed needles so the former BM could continue the campaign. Thus, the crowd would be exponentially inoculated with each stick until the BIGLY Virus was finally eradicated by herd immunity.

The first person to whom Lakshmi administered the shot was none other than her former mentor, Mark Question. Upon receiving the vaccine, he responded in a feminine voice, "Oh my goodness! I've been so infected with hate, hypocrisy, and lies! The BIGLY Virus was eating away my body and soul! I now recognize the error of my ways. 'Tis better to love than to hate. Better to give than receive. Better to be your true authentic self rather than some artificial construct that society demands of you. I now identify as Mary Kwest. Thank you, Lakshmi, for saving me!" Then, with her characteristic zeal, Mary Kwest went about her new mission of jamming a needle into every arm she could find.

At first, MISTER BIGLY was oblivious to the upheaval below. He was under the mistaken impression that the commotion in the crowd was a rabid reaction to his inspiring remarks. MISTER BIGLY had long prided himself on his ability to "read the room," but in this case, his instincts sorely failed him. At approximately the "time" he thought he had his Minions whipped into a fevered pitch, the fever broke. The mayhem he witnessed was not the adulation he imagined; rather, it was the spectacle of BIGLY's former-Minions scurrying right-side-up to inoculate any upside-down virus sufferer whose arms they could get their hands on.

"As I was saying," he continued, trying to rein in his flock, "buy my BIGLY's Bill of Goods! Only $199.99! But wait! There's more! Buy it today and I'll throw in a copy of my book: MISTER BIGLY's Art of the Steal! You can have my book free if you buy my Bill of Goods for just $299.99! That I can tell you! Believe me!"

It finally dawned on MISTER BIGLY that he was losing his grip. This had never happened before. He was on uncharted territory. He pulled out a litany of his greatest hits to no avail.

"Wait!" he cried. "Come back! I'm not through talking yet! I'm a *winner*! Buy my Bill of Goods and *win*! Destroy the Others and *win*! Pizza Pedophile! Remember Pizza Pedophile Sophia Wise? Wait! Where's everybody going?"

But it was too late. Herd immunity had been reached. The BIGLY Virus had dissipated, and with the virus went the mob. They didn't storm the tower for revenge. Nor did they hurl rotten tomatoes, throw him off the balcony, or ride him out of town on a rail. No, for sages have said that the opposite of love is not hate, but indifference. And indifference is what the crowd showed MISTER BIGLY. He no longer had anything of interest to them, so they simply shrugged their shoulders, turned their backs, and walked home on their own two feet.

"Lakshmi sighed and watched Sophia lean lazily against an old maple tree."

20. THE RIVER OF TRUTH

While Lakshmi and Sophia discuss weighty subjects, Special Ed injects his perspective; Special Ed leads Lakshmi and Sophia to the River; Sophia departs, leaving Lakshmi to complete her journey.

"SO, DID YOU EVER find the River of Truth?"

Sophia sat on a river bank with Lakshmi, eating carrots and hummus from a picnic spread before them. They watched Special Ed frolicking in the water, making up games with the geese and ducks that happened by.

"I don't know, Sophia. I keep feeling somebody is up there tossing clues on my head and saying, '*Now* do you get it?' And I say to He, She, Them, It, or however He/She/Them/It identifies, 'I think I'm close. Just give me one more clue.' "

Lakshmi sighed and watched Sophia lean lazily against an old maple tree. A sign was nailed to the tree, directly above her head. It read:

RIVER OF TRUTH

Special Ed happily bounded from the river, looking for someone to shake his waterlogged body off on. He found Lakshmi and Sophia and gave himself a vigorous rattle, feeling it only right to share his good fortune with them.

"Oh, Special Ed!" they protested simultaneously. Wiping the spray from their faces, they watched Special Ed roll on his back, kick his legs in the air, and smile with his entire body.

"Special Ed just had the most magnificent moment!" he exclaimed. "I swam in the cold cold river and I felt so alive!"

Lakshmi and Sophia followed Special Ed out of the corner of their eyes and listened out of the corner of their ears, but they were distracted by the weight of their conversation.

"Excuse us, Special Ed," said Lakshmi, "but we have many important issues to discuss."

"Discuss, discuss, discuss," said Special Ed. He sprinted along the river bank, better to feel the wind in his face.

Sophia attempted to pick up the thread of their conversation. "Do you think MISTER BIGLY will actually go to jail?"

Lakshmi: "I don't know, but even if he does, there will always be a new MISTER BIGLY."

Sophia: "Isn't that the truth? And his Minions will get conned all over again."

Lakshmi: "You know the old saying: Fool me once, shame on you; fool me twice and I'm a proud citizen of the Free Nation."

Special Ed stood on the bank, facing the river, and barked like the dog he was. It felt good to bark good and loud and tell everybody Special Ed was here.

Sophia: "In the meantime, the planet is warming, the seas are rising, there's more plastic in the ocean than there are fish, and more people on the planet than there are rats."

Lakshmi: "There are still more cockroaches than people."

"And now Special Ed is having another magnificent moment!" proclaimed Special Ed. "It's so wonderful to roll in the grass, scratch my back, and dry it at the same 'time!' Most assuredly!"

Sophia changed the subject. "I wonder how we can find our way back to Red Rock from here."

"Good question," said Lakshmi. "I think we lost the trail."

"Aren't you misremembering something?" Special Ed had finished rolling and was busying himself sniffing the ground where he'd peed.

"Yes," said Sophia, "we forgot how to find our way home."

"But you erased something," said Special Ed. "You misremembered that Special Ed has an excellent smeller. I'll show you the way."

Lakshmi and Sophia looked at each other in recognition.

Lakshmi's thought molecules had given Special Ed a monk's robe.

"But first, I must train you for your journey. To find your way home, you must have a swim in the river."

Along with the monk attire, Lakshmi's thought molecules gave Special Ed a leash to hold in his mouth. The leash split two ways at the end and hooked to collars around Lakshmi and Sophia's necks. Special Ed led them to the river, released them from their collars, and instructed them to undress. Once they'd done so, he pranced circles around them and shouted, "Last one in is a BIGLY Minion!"

Lakshmi and Sophia certainly didn't want to be BIGLY Minions, so into the river they plunged.

*

Holding hands, they slid headlong into the depths. The water carried no weight, imposed no resistance to their effortless descent. The river's cold thrilled Lakshmi to the bone, removed all thoughts of anything beyond the moment, and made every cell in her body stand up and shout, "I'm alive!"

"This must be what it feels like to be Special Ed," she thought.

Sophia felt it too. Together, they performed an elaborate water dance, darting in and out of fish schools who, in turn, flitted above, below, and around them. But their celebration turned solemn when they understood they were not becoming one with the fish; they were foreigners in a foreign land. The fish they swam amongst were on a sober quest to procreate and survive. They were all business. Salmon bustling up river to spawn; trout trolling for food; minnows trying not to be eaten. And everyone guarding against humans and their countless variations on the dispensation of doom.

No, Lakshmi and Sophia were not welcome here. At best, they were a nuisance; at worst, a terror to be avoided at any cost. As they frolicked among the fish, Lakshmi's thought molecules briefly turned her and Sophia into tourists sporting tropical shirts, khaki shorts, and cameras strapped around their necks. They found themselves back in the Land of the Others, being welcomed by their sacred ritual dance. Lakshmi and Sophia barged right in and danced clumsily along, spilling the margaritas they waved drunkenly over their heads. The puzzled Others tried to maintain a polite distance as they continued their ceremony. Then Lakshmi and Sophia were once again swimming naked among the fish who, like the Others, gave a wide berth to these alien sightseers. Best to move on.

So they descended:
into midnight silence
into vacuum
into void
into dimension beyond "time"
beyond words
beyond conscience or will.

Beyond dreams
beyond black
beyond white
beyond rainbows
beyond matter, moment, or care...

Sophia said, "I must leave now."

Lakshmi: "Why?"

Sophia: "I've done what I came to do. I released you from
MISTER BIGLY's clutches. I accompanied you to the depths
of the river. Now I must depart your dream and return
to Red Rock where there's much to be done. And you,
Lakshmi, are near the end of your journey. You must finish
what you set out to do. Alone."

"Goodbye, Sophia. I hope to see you in Red Rock someday."

With that, Sophia kissed Lakshmi—a lover's kiss—and
swam upward and out of sight, leaving Lakshmi alone at the
bottom of the watery abyss.

*

She hears the drums. The same drums that ushered in the
beginning of her voyage. The same staccato wave of congas that
begin in the far distance and, once again, methodically approach.
The indigenous chants. The painted faces. The jewels, the beads,
the bones. The eyes. Here they come again.

The sinewy arms. Reaching hands. Dancing torsos. "We see you,"
they say again. "We see you."

The insistent rhythm. The willful gestures. The purposeful intent.
The powerful mix of brown faces, boneless bodies, ancestral
voices calling, singing, howling, roaring in tandem with drums
that beat so deafeningly close they penetrate Lakshmi's brain and
pound from inside out. A thousand hands lift Lakshmi and offer her
up to the musical thunder. She levitates, her body abandoned. Her
conscience disintegrates into her naked soul.

Light. What is the color of light? Is it gold? Is it white? Is it opposite of night? Lakshmi's thought molecules explode into light and she becomes light and light becomes her. No love no hate no fear no pain. No yes. No no. Light is all.

Visions blink in the light. Galileo becomes Einstein becomes Hawking. A flash of star-studded universe. Rod Serling explains.

Each star a grain in a vast desert. Sage and sand. Junipers and snakes. Chameleon darts among rust-colored mushroom-shaped rocks piled high. Ancient grizzled Don Juan beams a broken-tooth, stained-tooth smile. Offers Lakshmi a mushroom.

"Eat," he says.

"No thanks," she says. "I have no want. I have no need."

No want. No need.

Indigenous spirits coax. "We see you. Come. Fall into us. Come. We will hold you. Come. We see you. We love you. Come."

They carry her eight miles high. Mother Earth below. Wounded warrior. Burnt, bent, beleaguered, battle-scarred sphere. Dry brown weeping planet. Littered with butts. Littered with wrappers. Littered with plastic bags, plastic bottles, plastic caps, plastic straws. Litter piled eight miles high.

Littered with Others crawling, clamoring, climbing a wall that keeps them out of Rich Man's yard. Rich Man pumps oil from the Others' village, fills up vats at the top of the wall, pours it down on their heads. Sign says, "Keep out."

Mass migration. Animals of every design stampede on a suffering planet in a breathing universe, searching for food, searching for water, searching for a place they can live. Climb on Noah's Ark. The Ark is a Trojan horse.

Breathing universe. Expands—contracts—expands—contracts. Birth—death—birth—death. Where does this cycle begin—end—begin—end?

Breathing universe speaks: "If every star is but a grain of sand, then what are you, Lakshmi Jackson? And if you are but an atom in relation to a star, then what is an atom in relation to *you*? A universe unto itself? Just asking."

Out from the breathing universe, Jack Nicholson as Colonel Jessup bellows: "You can't handle the truth!"

Jack Nicholson morphs into Fred Rogers saying: "Discovering the truth about ourselves is a lifetime's work, but it's worth the effort."

Mr. Rogers becomes the Buddha: "Three things cannot be long hidden: the sun, the moon, and the truth."

The Buddha becomes the Dalai Lama: "Be kind whenever possible. It is always possible."

The Dalai Lama becomes John Lennon: "All you need is love."

Lakshmi breathes with the breathing universe. Weeps for her father, Ben Jackson, aka: The Roadside Slaughterer, gunned down from the roof of the FreeCorps building. Weeps for her mother, Aruna; weeps for her suffering. Weeps for her strength. Weeps for a world in labor: its pain, its cruelty, its wondrous beauty and vibrant life.

Here come Philbert and Hazel Brain, bouncing on their heads as they emerge from the Hospital for the Ironically Challenged. Dr. Drole, Dr. Farse, and the inmates pour out, babbling ironically. Here come Wendell Smarm and the entire Classical Orators League, reciting in unison the Serenity Prayer: "…grant me the serenity to accept the things I cannot change…" while Pachelbel's Canon plays in the background. Here come the four wise wolves, going about their wild ways, pleading for understanding. Lance Lovesalot steps out of Metaphor Hotel, leans forward and plants a tender kiss on Lakshmi's open lips. He pats her belly where their baby grows.

Mark **Question** leaps forward leading his Death Metal band of **Questionables**. With a flick of his tongue, he morphs into Mark **Question**, radio jockey/caveman. With one swift crash of his giant club, he decimates Metaphor Hotel, grows a beard, dons elk horns, and brandishes an assault rifle. He grovels at the feet of MISTER BIGLY who, standing behind bars and dressed in an orange jumpsuit, waves his MISTER BIGLY's Bill of Goods and offers to sell it at the bargain price of just $399. Lakshmi absent-mindedly rubs her perfect skipping rock and reflects upon it all.

She lays her head in Grandma Una's lap as Una lovingly strokes her hair. She looks up and there are her ancient guides, bidding her farewell and sending her home. There is Sophia Wise, smiling down upon her, gently playing her mandolin. And there is Special Ed, standing at the water's edge, happily drinking from the River of Truth.

EPILOGUE

LAKSHMI AWOKE from her dream. She found herself still lying in the Boat of Bob, the sun still beating down on her and the boat and the placid sea. She blinked and yawned, lazy and content. She seemed to remember some hazy pictures on the tip of her brain, but she wasn't able to access them. Whatever motive had compelled her to travel on this journey had now dissipated. The sun would set before long. Sophia needed all the help she could get in Red Rock. "Time" to go home.

She looked up. To her wonderment, at the opposite end of the boat sat Special Ed. He had been watching her patiently. When she saw him, he wagged his tail and smiled with his tongue dripping out of his mouth.

"WOOF WOOF!" he cried enthusiastically.

Lakshmi knew that if he could speak English, he would have said, "Special Ed is so happy to see you! Most assuredly!"

He bounded across the boat and smothered her with kisses. Once his greeting was complete, he began sniffing her tummy with rapt curiosity. Something was going on in there. Lakshmi rubbed her belly and felt the new life growing inside her. Although she knew not where this life had come from, she was not surprised.

So many mixed feelings about bringing a child into this cruel and chaotic world. She feared the horrors her daughter (and she knew it was a daughter) would be subjected to. And yet, she thought, "Life goes on. I will do all I can to arm this little girl with power and knowledge so she may rise above whatever challenges come her way. I will arm her with love and wisdom so she may add her weight to all that is good. I will name her Hope."

Lakshmi's hand fidgeted in her pants pocket and felt something solid. She reached in and pulled out the most perfect skipping rock she'd ever seen. She did not remember the day she found it with Special Ed, nor had she any idea how it got there. She only knew, somewhere in the back of her mind, she'd been saving this perfect skipping rock for the perfect occasion.

She held it in her hand, felt its perfectly buffed smoothness, its perfect circular shape, the heft of it just right. She stood up in the boat and surveyed the ocean which she determined to be smooth as glass. She hesitated. Then, in this perfect moment, on this perfect day, on this perfect sea, Lakshmi made a wish and flung her perfect skipping rock, and watched it skip a thousand skips before it sank beneath the surface and disappeared.

ᏮᎻᎬ ᎬᏁᎠ

About the Author

Paul Chasman has gone through several incarnations in his 70-plus years. He is a lifelong guitarist with over 20 albums to his credit. In 2003, after George W. Bush invaded Iraq, Carl Estrada inhabited Paul's body and, through Paul, Carl has written over 2000 letters of "Advice and Constructive Criticism to the Famous, the Infamous, and the Current Administration." Paul completed his reincarnation as an author in 2004 when he wrote *The Book of Bob*. *Lakshmi and the River of Truth* is the long-awaited sequel. Paul lives with his wife, two dogs, and two cats at an undisclosed location.

www.paulchasmanbooks.com
www.thecarlletters.com
www.paulchasmanguitar.com
Twitter: @chasman_paul
Bay View Arts
P.O. Box 657
Washougal, WA 98671

Special thanks to Jim Breithaupt, Tom Robertson, Byron Schimpp, and Rolf Priebe. And thank you every day of my life to my wife, Anna Wiancko Chasman.

About the Illustrator

A life-long resident of the Portland Oregon area, Jerry Kruger attained a bachelor's degree in graphic design from Portland State University in 1969. His career as a designer and illustrator began in 1971 after extensive travels in Europe that year. Illustrations have appeared in numerous local and regional publications since the early 1980's, including *Willamette Week, The Oregonian, Oregon Magazine, Northwest Energy News* and many others. Jerry designed Paul Chasman's first two albums in 1979 and 1980. Jerry Kruger lives in Southwest Portland with his wife Pam.

Made in the USA
Middletown, DE
23 October 2021